PRAISE FOR

IN THE DARK

"A lyrical, richly textured novel of great beauty and depth that pulses with humanity and love amid the heartbreak and desolation of war. Such resonant, layered storytelling from a writer of unique sensibility. This story of two sisters and the wonderful cast of fully inhabited characters will stay with me a long time. A graceful, impactful, insightful read."

Lisa Harding

"*In the Dark* is a heart-breaking, fiercely honest and formally daring novel, which richly rewards attentive reading. Anamaría Crowe Serrano is a poet whose prose carries over poetry's intensities, with her eye and ear for significant detail, expressed in short, dense, highly-charged chapters. It is set at an exceptionally grim moment in Spain's grim Civil War, during the Francoist siege of a rather reluctantly Republican town in Teruel. Crowe's relentless but authentic portrayal of the brutality and venality of leftist, as well as fascist, militants is challenging, at least for those of us who hold a special place for Spain's Second Republic in our hearts and minds. But good fiction should challenge us. This novel does not carry a flag for any political creed, but only for the endurance of human kindness and human love in the face of unbearable human cruelty. The central characters, especially the women, are drawn with convincing empathy. The plot is very tightly wound, twisting at the very end in a way that is likely to make you gasp— and send you straight back to the beginning for a second read."

Paddy Woodworth

"This tells the story of how men all but destroy Spain during its Civil War but the women waiting at home hold the country's jagged pieces together. This is historical fiction with the pulse of life in it."

Martina Devlin

"A stellar and compelling Spanish Civil War novel-cum-love story, which has already earned its place on our bookshelves beside Ernest Hemingway's For Whom the Bell Tolls. Told through the eyes of two combative sisters under the one roof – Maria and Julita – whose partners are fighting on opposite sides of the conflict, we see the impact of the warfare both upon their children and a handful of fellow townspeople, including a saintly doctor, who arrive to shelter with them. That all are victims of this war – as all are of any war – is but a portion of the wisdom within these pages, nor will readers need ask for whom the bells toll at the end. Never mind an ending which bequeaths more than a sting – something more like a whiplash – to a mighty tale."

Anthony Glavin

"*In the Dark* reads like a polyphonic prose poem, but don't be fooled, this is a tense, psychological thriller. Set during the Spanish Civil War, in a besieged household as divided as the warring factions outside, there's a surprise at the end you won't see coming. It'll drive you back to the start to read the novel all over again."

Mary Morrissey

"Anamaría Crowe Serrano has written a remarkable novel. *In The Dark* is an extraordinary and vivid reading experience, one that will remain with every reader for quite some time after the final page is turned. Giving the reader this incredible insight into the Spanish Civil War from the female perspectives of María, Julita and other women, *In The Dark* is historically immersive and quite a special novel."

Mairéad Hearne, Swirl and Thread

"In a country whose tortuous path toward democracy is built on the foundations of a 'Great Forgetting,' it is unsurprising that so much is still kept in the dark. In her début novel, Anamaría Crowe Serrano is writing not just to the fisherman, farmer or peasant at work, but to the women in those same hills: the sisters, the mothers, the daughters and the wives who were left to reap the harvest. Unprotected by the order of privilege, they are dragged by the hair into the theatre war. Too often considered minor characters, these women must wake every single morning to the bombs dropping and the mortar shells whizzing about their ears and rely solely on the human need to survive.

Crowe Serrano guides the spotlight way from those who manage the war and onto those who manage in a war, held in domestic prisons from which there no escape. This is a difficult light that illuminates our too-easily come by assumptions about war, about civil war; assumptions based on so much that was kept in the dark.

Through a gap in the stairs, Anamaría Crowe Serrano allows a chink of light to illuminate – amid the blood, the dust and the crumbling debris – the lives of characters that for too long have been kept in the dark. She probes all your assumptions about right and wrong, about taking sides."

Keith Payne

"…the novel sinks its teeth into you – addressing the blinding nature of ideology, the tensions between sisters, and the weight of forbidden love."

Carrie Callaghan Historical Novels Review

IN THE DARK

ANAMARÍA CROWE SERRANO

IN THE DARK

First published 2021

Turas Press,

6-9 Trinity Street,

Dublin D02 EY47

ISBN: 978-1-913598-16-7

Ebook Kindle

ISBN: 978-1-913598-17-4

Ebook Kobo

ISBN: 978-1-913598-23-5

Cover design by Angie Crowe

Interior Typesetting by Printwell Design, Dublin 3

Printed in Ireland by

SPRINTprint

Also by Anamaría Crowe Serrano

TURAS PRESS

Crunch

CORRUPT PRESS

KaleidoGraph

one columbus leap

SHEARSMAN BOOKS

^{on}Words and ^{up}Words

Femispheres

EMPIRÌA

Paso Doble

TRANSLATIONS

(Shearsman)

Beyond the Sea, by Elsa Cross

(Gradiva Publications)

Stone Green, by A. Toni

Poetic Dialogue with T.S. Eliot's Four Quartets, by L. Celi

Selected Poems, by D. Raimondi

(amazon.com)

Killing Pythagoras, by M. Chicot

(Chelsea Editions)

Paradigm: New and Selected Poems, by A. de Palchi

Mindskin, by A. Zagaroli

Other Signs, Other Circles, by A. Ferramosca

Instructions on How to Read a Newspaper, by V. Magrelli

(Edizioni del Leone)

Porte/Doors, by Annamaria Ferramosca

para María y Félix

quienes me enseñaron a escribir

History is a nightmare from which I am trying to awake

James Joyce

Bar Joselito. The bustle and Joselito's widow, Encarna, are one and the same thing. Encarna is tables and chairs. She is indoors, outdoors, shutters open, sawdust, chalkboard. She is tinkling glasses, barrels and rolling laughter. She is the centre of the village square, Plaza del Torico, fulcrum of joy and sorrow. Fabric well woven. Encarna holds everything and everyone together. Which is a problem if one thread snags.

María helps out. In Joselito's day, the clientele changed slowly, following the pace of natural lives. But with war, familiarity goes. People disappear, like María's husband, Ramón, and her sister's husband, Antonio. Bar stools are filled by Republican troops whose town this is not, but whose uniform gives licence to belong. From behind the bar María observes them and in each one's paunch, shoulders, face, she sees a father, brother, son.

A smile can convey solidarity. Sometimes politeness. Often when these men smile at her, it is desperation, even arrogance. Mostly she wishes they wouldn't smile. She thinks of Ramón, his parting kiss as he left for the front, his squeeze so tight she couldn't breathe. Breathing is hard even now when she thinks of him. He is on the other side—with the military. Not entirely by choice, but the situation had become chaotic. They came for him, the men some call rebels, fascists, and who knows what they'd have done if he had refused.

The things she cannot say about him, she rubs and rubs into the glasses in the sink. There are so many things now that people mustn't say.

Every task she performs in the bar is meticulous—chairs, floor, counter, shelves, food, drink. The more meticulous her work the better it hides her fear.

Puzzling, the postman's news. He says the rebels have turned things around and gained some ground on the Republicans. What to make of that. In only a matter of weeks.

Fascist troops now sit in the bar. And these, María observes, are the same as the others. Fathers, sons, brothers.

They drink the same. Laugh the same. At the enemy pushed into the hills.

She wonders about Ramón. She could ask them, but best not engage with any of these men.

They mention Franco. He will send reinforcements, they say confidently. If the Republicans on the hills haven't frozen to death in the meantime.

Joselito's has a clear view of everything that goes on in Plaza del Torico. María and Encarna could turn away but the attraction of death is inexplicable. Maybe watching is an act of defiance. Maybe it's solidarity with the dead. Besides, they don't know this is the beginning, before everything else, and no one imagines death on their doorstep.

People are gathering. Moments before the slaughter they see the Hunchback and the prisoner coming from the direction of the seminary, where Franco's military are now holding prisoners. Those who couldn't retreat fast enough to the hills.

Crowds give events an air of fanfare. You'd think there was going to be a party but silence spreads as the Hunchback and the prisoner arrive. María and Encarna hardly have time to blink before they realise what's happening. By the fountain six shots to the legs and he falls to the ground. The Hunchback stands over him. He won't, they gasp, incredulous. This is the village square. Decent people. But his agenda is not theirs. He puts his pistol to the man's head. Purposefully. Is it a mercy. Out of his agony then, and the Hunchback walks away.

From the shock of bullets to the reflex of habit. María blesses herself. *Que en paz descanse.* May he rest in peace. The village swarms around the dead man. Why does no one remove him. What are they waiting for. Behind the window, María and Encarna cling to each other.

The Hunchback returns, this time with a line of men. Now the professor tied to the mayor of Mora and now the mayor of Mora tied to the insurance salesman and now the insurance salesman tied to the civil engineer and now the civil engineer tied to.

The legs. The head. One of them, who, writhing on the ground, cries out *Viva la República*. They hear it and a thick carpet of blood creeps across the square. To the door.

Encarna has to sit. María too. Cautiously they ease themselves onto chairs as if it is the first time they have ever sat on a chair. They watch people in the square search for loved ones among the dead. Hours pass and suddenly darkness descends.

For Julita it boils down to this: Brunete, July 1937. The river is flowing. Spray and mud and marching in mud. They are retreating from the rebel attack. Hastily, scrambling for safety. Six months of no respite from Franco's advances, and every manoeuvre is harder, every route longer. The slaughter more swift, although that is much debated.

At home she imagines the taste of minerals in the river, the taste of forests and mountains feeding into it. She imagines him, Antonio, getting ready to cross. One of many. Where were the others. Was there no one to grab hold of him.

Holding the pack high, rifle higher, Antonio pushes towards the far bank in the chain of men. Was there no bridge, she wants to ask. Could they not... The force of the river easily washes the questions from her tongue. Not that she would ask. To question might be considered disloyal to the Republic, and that is something she is not.

One after the other the men wade, calibrating body weight this way, that, as feet fumble for purchase under the water. And then his next step. The one that plays endlessly in Julita's mind. Did a rock shift underfoot. Was it his balance. He must have summoned sight, sound, everything he had until there was nothing left. He would fight to the end, wouldn't he. For her. For the boys.

She imagines his comrades making futile attempts to hold on to him. Slippery. Another attempt, grabbing at a strap, a hand. He never learnt to swim. Surely, someone. Round and round in her head until the shouting settles into disbelief.

A river smells no fear. Hears no plea. A river just is. Indiscriminately, it will take a man.

Sometimes the road to work is not just that. María has known this for months, since the road became an intimate part of her grief. She takes this stretch every day on her way to the bar. This turn, here, is the hardest, where she last…

If only Ramón hadn't been at the front she would have felt less alone.

It's unsafe, everyone had been saying for a week. There are soldiers everywhere. But she stumbled on. She needed doctor García, willed him to appear, pressing the child to her chest. Listless, pale Inés.

The child's face is everywhere every day on that stretch. Weight in her arms. She knew—Inés—she'd never—Inés—never—Inés— make it to the doctor—Inés. Pink lips purpling at her empty breast. Milk that had turned to drought for almost two weeks. Child to corpse. Her grief scripted in a letter for Ramón, so far away. Words that were painful to write.

In the five minutes to town this morning, the road is changing again. At first, claps of gunfire in the distance might account for it. The wretched heat of August, perhaps. The road seems to have forgotten who she is, recoiling into hollows under her feet, rolling into the ditch.

In the turmoil of road disappearing—Inés disappearing—she sees it from the corner of her eye. A face among the brambles. A cry.

Did it come from her or from the grasses burning in the sun. How can it be him. Skin, bone, eyes, fear.

María, he calls, my love, it's me.

Paralysed, she watches him stir, part the brambles. A cautious leg, emaciated. How…, she begins, I thought…

Their words of many months ago stick to her in the heat. If she would hide him should he manage to escape. Yes, she said. Whatever the risk, never thinking it would really happen. Now, the burden of it almost makes her want to run. If only everything would end, she thinks, staring at him in the ditch as if she is seeing a ghost. But it is the job of the living to survive.

María, he repeats. It is an effort for him to speak but she can read his eyes. They speak of love, innocence, blame, heat, the empty house even when it's full. So much we will never understand, she thinks. We may not be here in a few months. He does not deserve to be shot for desertion.

My dearest, she goes to him, to touch, dispel the dream. I'll come for you tonight, she says, when it's dark. Can you wait a little longer.

Hours later, in the dark, she learns more about his eyes. They can speak even when they're closed. The closed eyes of a man in a ditch who has forsaken his cause in the war, holding fast to failing breath, to what's left of integrity. No one is right, the eyes say. Least of all me.

On the pew after Mass, María thinks of loyalty. How choosing one side or the other does not always imply loyalty. Cold wood and incense creep up her skirt. She presses her knees tighter. God creeps up her skirt. *Dios te salve María*. Hail Mary.

I could disappear, he had suggested, tentatively, before leaving. Except, where to—the attic, under the stairs. A darkness no one would understand. An act of cowardice. But we mustn't judge.

You know I've always loved you, he said before he left. *Llena eres de gracia*. Full of grace.

As if to bolster the idea, one of the men from Sagunto disappeared into rumour shortly after the war began. It's easier for a village to swallow the darkness when there's a rumour of light. That invisible man will win the war yet, the villagers still laugh because there is nothing else to laugh about. Where did he go, they shake their heads. Is he actually gone.

Would you help me, he asked. That was light years ago, but María shivers now at the recollection. God is watching and to dream is one thing. Still…

Would you help me. It would have to be our secret.

The olives in Sagunto were ripe last year and by dawn they had been picked even though there were no hands. A miracle, everyone said. The man's wife never even smiled. *Bendita tu eres*… Blessed art thou… Again this year the olives are ready and the sunflower petals have started to fall. María's lips are sealed.

And how many other lips, she wonders, *entre todas las mujeres.* Amongst women. Now she is sure she knows how the olives in Sagunto get picked in the night. *Bendito el fruto.* Blessed is the fruit. Sometimes, when nothing makes sense, we call it a miracle. And sometimes, when it makes perfect sense, it's also useful to call it a miracle.

Into mists and rivers and holes in the ground, the men are gone, small pieces of them carried away by the forest, by the thoughts of others. No, she said. It will never work. Go serve your country. I couldn't live with myself.

Now he is back she cannot refuse. *Ruega por nosotros.* Pray for us. There is only one way to deal with this. A risk for both of them. A risk with serious consequences. *Pecadores.* Sinners. But maybe it can work. Maybe. There are many ways to live a life, she thinks.

There are coffins and there are coffins.

Little Inés in a small white box.

Living, breathing, he measures the space under the stairs. This is her solution.

No one will find you here.

It will do even though it's no more than a large box. He wonders how he will live or breathe. He, a man of the fields, forfeiting soil and sun. Who knows how long, this stifling wait.

As long as it takes, María says. A few months at most. I am here for you.

The night he entered the box he clutched her arm. She thought of Inés, the small white box, how she clutched the child. She thought of the sadness of soil under the ground.

Your sister must never find out. Not a word to Julita, I beg you. Or the children. No one.

As if she would.

Three paces from the back wall and he can no longer stand. Muscle wastes. From standing, the stairs descend above his head. Reality descends every time María or the children go up or down. Three paces from the bricked wall that used to be open to the kitchen. At the narrow wedge of his box are food, candles, a pot for ablutions. One for waste. He can lie full length, head touching the back wall, feet touching the bottom of the stairs. What more does a man need. To stand. To sit. To sleep. To sit. To stand. To sit. To cramp. To stand. To sleep.

To breathe.

Eye level, squinting through the crack. A crack in a wall used to be a defect. Now every time he looks through it he dwells on its redeeming nature. Vital possibilities of defects. María's hair just within view at the table as she shakes her head when Tomás asks where his father is. He's fighting in the war, she says. Your father's a brave man.

When Julita or Manolo visit he worries they will hear his heart thumping. There are only ribs and a thin layer of skin between it and the flimsy brick wall.

so this is the solution—buried alive

they spoke of hell from the pulpit on Sundays—as if they knew—
as if flames were the ultimate horror—but they're not

I think of the boys—Fernando and José—boys only just men—
gone for so long—how it must be for Julita without them—for
Manolo without his brothers

I think of little Inés—as if being entombed here is an atonement
for her death—so many deaths—innocent children—this is what
it's like—we kill life one way or another

María hasn't mentioned the baby—it's too raw so I don't bring it
up—not yet—though there are so many things I would like to
know

how it happened—how she coped—how is it possible to feel so
close to someone you've never seen

I bite my tongue—about this—about other things

Julita is troubled by questions she doesn't ask. It was one thing for Antonio to be drafted in February. Another thing for their sons, Fernando and José, to enlist one month later. Then the official letter in August. Signed, Indalecio Prieto. Minister of Defence.

Like food in these times, paper is a luxury. Sheets discolour with the years but the text is official, written to remain: date, name, battalion, condolence. She presses the letter to her chest. These words about her husband, penned by strangers, are proof of something. That he gave his life for a better Spain.

The words keep swimming every time she reads them. Antonio. Drowned.

boredom—enough to drive a man insane

it helps to think of the night sky—all the constellations from Juanjo's conversations—what happened to him—so many comrades I will never see again

you can always find your way home he said—at night—and I did—it was almost as if he knew I'd need to some day

Ursa Major and Polaris—field after field—in ditches or among grasses lying low I could follow those stars—clinging to the constellations to distract me from the mosquitoes and the terror of being caught

onwards—Orion with his bright belt and his hunting dog—Canis Major with the brightest star in the sky—I see it stretched across the night's path—faithful companion—I talked so much to that one—eighty-eight constellations Juanjo used to say—even though we can't see them all—but they're there—and here in my head

if only I had thought about it—had a plan for the future—north would have been better—into the forests—maybe to France

but all I thought of was home—the immediacy of fleeing

and instead I climbed into a tomb

The women kill the long evenings with cards. Since Ramón left for the war, María's door is always open. People think it's because she's lonely now, but they're wrong. Even if they asked, she could never tell. They hear her talking aloud when there's no one around, but no one has the heart to say what they really think. Not even Julita, always quick to say what's on her mind.

The women have many reasons for coming to María's house. Julita for the gossip. And to keep an eye on what her sister is doing. Lips bright red despite the black of mourning. Encarna for company when she's not at the bar. Eyebrows plucked into shape. She worries about María, the daughter she never had. Manolo has no reason. He just does what his mother tells him, so he believes he has his father's and his brothers' shoes to fill. If this is a burden, he wears it lightly, though it is hard to imagine him ever being man of the house. Quiet, withdrawn, part of him comes for his cousins, Alicia and Tomás. The opposites of quiet and withdrawn.

That husband of yours should have been home on leave by now, Julita says, picking a card from the deck. She refuses to name him, in the silent way of rancour. Her little sister got the dashing man, the one with charm, whereas Julita got the first one who came along. Embarrassed to be unmarried at twenty-three.

Ramón, María says under her breath, which is misunderstood for sadness.

Julita twists the blade. Unless he's found somewhere else to go. Pass. Some of them, cowards, desert.

Encarna gently interjects. Julita, no one has deserted. Ramón will come back when he gets leave. I've heard they are much needed at the front. They are fighting without leave for many months. Your own boys are in the same position. What is it now, eight months.

Ten, she corrects.

There are explanations for bitterness, of course there are. Some go back far. Losing Antonio in the summer and her boys swallowed by the war must account for some of it. Still, it's hard to put up with her jibes. Hard to accept she did nothing to help when Inés was so ill. This is what it means to be poisoned by despair.

María bites her tongue. Something deep inside us all is breaking but there is nothing anyone can do. He certainly can't come out now from his hiding place under the stairs. He can't even go somewhere else. There is nowhere to hide.

I think of comrades slaughtered on the battle field—shot for attempting to flee—crammed into dungeons they will never survive

I think of their families as I watch mine through the hole in the wall

I think of torture

I think of this cramped space—not knowing if I will get out or what will happen if I do

I think of everything that is lost in confinement

I think that the impossible has come to pass—war has made us invisible—once we were alive and now we have simply ceased to be—a waste of lives

I think of being invisible in the middle of this room—how I have been spared

I think of Julita—her sharp tongue—scathing

I think of the baby—and María—darling sweet María

At times I think I am the luckiest man alive

Shh... How she loves is another story. What it means in these circumstances. Sometimes love is impossible. The children wake or her sister stays the night—increasingly—because she cannot bear to return to her own tomb.

But some nights everything settles. In summer everything except the crickets. So invisibly public.

I am here, she whispers as she passes the wall with the laundry. There is always a pretext to mumble as she passes the wall. Not knowing if she'll be heard.

It's complicated. Climbing the stairs. Stopping on each step. At the third, she bends to the fourth. Loose if you put pressure in just the right place, and down she slips. Blindly, feet first, dangling from the waist down, suppressing sound. Once inside, she pulls the step back into place above her, crawls to the back of the box where they can both stand.

In silence, their hands, their lips. María, he whispers, I'm afraid I might never get out of here. Afraid this is all there is for me.

Shh...

Last night he crawled out. The strangeness of a bed, he thinks. Of a body moving freely. Yielding its secrets. Hushed of necessity. This act of rebellion.

      [

                                    ]

[
]

[   ]   [

                     ]

   [   ] [   ]

[   ]   [   ]   [   ] [ ]

[ ] [ ] [ ] [ ][][][] [

    ] [Shh…, my love!]

The letters that arrive for María go into the chest of drawers in her bedroom. Dark wood for dark thoughts.

You say few things in your letter. I suppose there's no reason why you should tell me much. Food, lack of. Rats. Frostbite. The whir of gunfire. All these things you say, but you don't mention if you miss me. Between the lines, you're too busy. Busy helping everyone up there on the northern front. Busy staying alive, being practical, efficient. Why would you miss me. Remember the day I asked you what you'd do if I died in the war. You said 'nothing'. You'd get on with living. That was the best possible answer. I expect no less of you.

fodder these boys who thought they knew something of Spain—
fair and freckled—passion and ideals flaming in rebellious hair—
from so many places...

America—England—Ireland—Czechoslovakia—Germany—
France—Russia—Poland—Yugoslavia—Italy

their skin—blistered under the sun only to burn for real inside the
tanks

boys betrayed by ideals—by the Republic and its commanders—
I remember the lie—vehemently defending the lie at first because
I wanted it to be true—Brunete is ours—surely—Minister Azaña
himself said so—and in they sent us to defend it

nine of us for every one of them—weapons and armoured
vehicles—if we can't win this battle with all that arsenal and
manpower it will never happen—that's what they said—cocksure

white—flashes from across the plain—after the flash it takes one
second—nothing faster than the speed of light—then the sound
of your own flesh—pierced through—then the sound of fire

you are fodder I kept telling them—if you desert they will hunt
you down—you are fodder—if you desert they will hunt you
down—fodder—they will hunt you

round and round—to one after another I said it—you can be shot
in the front or shot in the back—your choice—but they will hunt
you down

It's hard to get anything done. Hard to move from one street to the next. Hard to think. Everything slows in the snow.

At home there is no bread. No potatoes. Just days and days of snow. In the bar this afternoon they said it has reached minus thirty. Worst winter on record. Thousands of troops defending the town, one man said, but to hell with the civilians whose town this is.

At the greengrocer's the queue gets longer. Food hard won. It takes patience and stamina to stand for over an hour in freezing temperatures. María with the rest of them quietly prays for silence because sirens and aerial bombardment will rip through the queue quicker than shells. Who is the patron saint of silence. If only she knew, her prayers might be answered.

Instead, this morning, a new commotion. Men running in the street, shouting. The queue scattered before anyone knew why. María sheltered in the doorway to the Town Hall.

What... What's... Why are...

They're getting close, someone said. The Republicans are fighting back. They're surrounding the town and will soon flush out the rebels holding out at the convent and the seminary.

Is it true. What will happen then. The only true thing was she lost her place in the queue and by the time she reached the grocer's again the shutters were down. How can they say we are winning.

pain and its many versions of hell

time is not time—day not day—night at all hours

trying to erase myself—not make a sound—stifle a sneeze or not clear my throat when they are in the room

pain of holding still for hours—unable to move properly—unable to speak

pain of muscle tightening—acid—is that what builds up—that's what Juanjo thought when we had to hold still for hours

these thoughts are not good company

deserting was easy after all—not knowing when or if I'll get out of here is the real hell—if anyone had told me six months ago that it would be longer than two or three months I would have chosen to stay at the front and face my fate

I would not have compromised her like this

trapped animal—worse than animal

what was it like she sometimes asks

when I fall silent she thinks it's too painful to recall but that's not it—the memory comes without forcing it—I fall silent because there is no way to describe it even when memory besieges me—when it would punch a fist through the wall and even relish the pain

Manolo tells his cousins that his brothers are at the front, winning the war. Fernando writes to me often, he tells them with an air of importance. They have ammunition to beat the fascists, food to keep going for a year, even though it will never come to that.

When they ask about José, he explains his middle brother away. Too busy fighting in Madrid, but he promised to show me how to fire a gun. This he says with gravitas.

It's strange to see him animated, hovering as he usually does on the margin of their games.

What will the children make of reality as they grow older. Their childhood has been so disrupted for a long time now. What prospects will they have with no schooling. Does anyone ever think of this when they start a war.

Trembling, her hands, as he takes the bowl of broth. Usually she passes it down through the open slat on the stairs, but tonight she has climbed in. Perhaps to make up for the meagre offerings. No more than water flavoured with sloe and rowan berries. She didn't even have an onion.

I'm sorry, it's disgusting, she says in a conciliatory tone. I thought I'd try something different from the usual rosemary and thyme flavoured broth, but this is worse.

He smiles, stroking her cheek. Anything you make is delicious. Thank you. Come, sit beside me.

The children have learnt not to complain, she sighs. Not too much, anyway. There are only a few litres of water left, she says, looking at the jug. I will have to send them out to collect snow.

Julita comes over at odd hours while you're out, he tells her.

To her stricken look, he shakes his head. No, she just looks in the cupboards, sits at the table and takes out the needles. She always loved her knitting, didn't she. It keeps her nerves in check. Now it has come into its own. Knitting for the troops. The infernal clickety click. I can't stand it when it's just her on the other side of the wall.

She moves closer and he is enveloped in lavender, her private world. He sets the bowl down.

How did this happen, she whispers, you and me.

It's a conversation they repeat sometimes because memory is what holds their truth in place.

I dropped in with my father, didn't I, he answers. He needed help with the olive picking.

Yes. It was a bright day. Not too cold for November, she remembers. And Julita refused to help because… I can't remember why she didn't come that day.

Because Julita was always the boss and stubborn as they come, he says, and they laugh quietly.

So I went to help with the harvest. And I don't know what happened, she nudges him with a smile.

You lost your grip on the basket and the olives went rolling all over the place. Hours' worth of picking.

Your father was none too pleased. But—

You did it deliberately, he grins as he always does at the recollection.

No I didn't, she prods him playfully.

Oh, I know you did, he repeats, so we'd have an excuse to stay behind and salvage whatever we could.

I did not, she protests, trying to stifle her laughter.

So I could see you crawling over the field on all fours. Picking the olives individually up off the ground. Wiggling your bum to tease me, he whispers in her ear. You did that deliberately too.

I did not, she squeezes his arm. I felt so stupid when you came up to me and handed me the spade. I think you'll find this more useful, you said, very seriously. She stops to stifle more laughter. The story is fresh no matter how many times they recall it, as if they were living it all over again. And it was the look on your face… I don't know, a bemused look under the seriousness, trying not to laugh at me or something. A gentleness or shyness in the way you were trying to preserve my dignity. That's what did it. That's when I fell for you.

And when I handed you the spade, he continues, and our fingers touched like they had never done before, even though we had known each other for quite a while.

Yes, she recalls, lightly stroking his fingers.

so unalike as sisters—I cringe to hear Julita's limited views—ideals yes—but she thinks no further than ideals—as if the cause and its ideals are stronger than the reality—stronger than its effects—she needs a cause the way she needs to keep her hands busy

war changes a man—what I believed then I disbelieve now—what I wanted then I don't want now—not if this is the consequence

if only I had been encouraged to read when I was young—but what does a man of the fields want with books—we had our long-held views—respected—our work in the fields was good work—to choose a different life would have been to turn my back on everyone and everything—on the way we had always lived—insult to father and mother

Julita—strident—grating on my ear—I hate to hear her hold Manolo back—for fear he'll feel ashamed in front of Alicia and Tomás—clever children—it will cause division between them she seems to think—always small-minded

María—mellow—he can learn at his own pace—just because he might not participate in the same way doesn't mean he won't learn something

Comfort is upstairs when everything downstairs overwhelms. Beside the letters in the top drawer, the two cardigans. One white, one yellow. They had ribbons looped round the cuffs, tied into tiny bows. The baby hated them. Rubbed and rubbed her fists, fought one tiny hand against the other until María removed the ribbons. A determined little one. Like her sister.

Such a senseless death. That makes it worse.

The drawer is bigger than the small white box, she thinks. Solace in these pretty things. Soft knits. Gold bangle. Matching booties in pale lemon. Baby brush for hair that wouldn't lie flat. So many things resist our efforts.

Like Julita's hero, La Pasionaria. A wild woman waving banners, shouting *No pasarán*. Better to die on your feet than live on your knees.

She picks up the last letter.

You mention her here, La Pasionaria. No business for a woman, this dirty war, though you are careful to point out that you are fighting it clean. Neat and tidy. I imagine your hair properly combed with the parting to the side. Oils and shaving foam. They must have run out by now.

Is it her tone you dislike. The fact that she dares to express an opinion. What would you do to her for that. Shout back. Push her down the stairs. I don't like her myself. She's unladylike. But some things need to be shouted or they will never be heard. Shouted with banners. Why did I not shout.

Rumours abound. Encarna, dear Encarna who is always thinking of everyone, warned not to venture near Plaza del Torico or anywhere south of town where the Republican troops entered. The seminary, she said, where the Nationalist rebels have been holding out for days, has been taken.

But. Oranges. Julita said someone had smuggled a cart into the square. She went on about the oranges until everyone was salivating. The things you can do with oranges. Juice, marmalade, conserves, flavouring for rice, garlands, beauty creams for your face. Remember the oranges in Sagunto last year. Tangy, sweet. And the relish Mamá used to make for rabbit. And remember and remember and oranges, oranges, oranges. Fear will be outdone by hunger. Oranges exotic amidst constant gunfire crackle. Seville. Bougainvillea. Winter feasts. If only. Every cell in María's body is bursting for fruit.

A town is a living thing, she thinks, her progress almost static through the rubble. But shops and houses here are no more than skeletons of buildings. A town is its people. Dies with its people. Wheezing, spluttering, crumbling to demise.

Every day there are decisions to be made that no one ever thought about before. Decisions about a foot defiantly protruding from under rubble, then part of a leg caked in blood. The rest of the body buried. The decision to stop, unearth whoever it is, check for signs of life. What then. Oranges, somewhere, will not wait. The foot rebukes her and she is ashamed, wishing she had never seen it. Ashamed she cannot stomach its twistedness. Ashamed that the thought of oranges could take precedence over the dignity she should be paying the dead. But the dead are dead.

Through the snow another woman struggles up to the foot, stifles something that might have been hope, trudges on. Before she knows it María is in Calle de los Olivos. Tears turned to ice burn her cheeks. No sign of oranges. Just Julita's voice in her head and the colours of Seville.

A ruse—was that it—so she could snoop around the house. Does Julita not care that something could happen to her now that the town is under siege. What would the children do then. Maybe Encarna would take them in. Though Encarna talks of leaving if she could. Surely Julita wouldn't deliberately...

gasping for air today

gspng

smtms ts hrd t brth

cn't brth

how did I end up here—how

it was Indalecio Prieto—cn't brth—he was a good socialist—his vision was what inspired me—not the murderous insanity they stumbled into—a better way forward—wasn't that what I signed up for

how then

cn't brth

The children see things differently. A handbasin blasted into the middle of the street is pleading to be rescued. Cracked and chipped, easily it slides to the patio behind the barber's shop. Jagged bits of mirror beckon, and lengths of floral curtain. The smallest things are alluring. The more broken and abandoned the better. The more they can make them their own. A pair of glasses, a comb. But what interests Manolo most is the cigarette butts. Whenever he's out, he scours the ground and pockets them. Trappings of sophistication.

Can we get a lighter somewhere, Manolo asks Tomás, retrieving another butt. How about over there. Or matches.

Whatever his older cousin says, Tomás will do. Everything feels safe and privileged with Manolo who is nearly a man.

Have the tent ready when we come back, he tells Alicia as they climb through the broken window frame into the sound of distant mortar bombs. Far enough away to pose no threat, their ears attuned to distance, unaware of their new skills.

María's house is bright this evening when others are in darkness. Sometimes it's the other way around. Who is the patron saint of electrical cables. He has interceded. The evening card games can continue. Along with the resentments.

I'm lucky we still have electricity in the bar, Encarna says. I hear that many—

You must tell us how you've arranged this, Julita cuts her off, eyeing María with exaggerated innocence and waving her hand overhead. How come no one else has light.

It's not really a question.

Yes they do, Encarna defends. The cables are sometimes unstable, that's all. The bar, too, as I said. Power is down in many places, but—

People do favours for things like that, Julita mulls, pursing her painted lips. The rebels do, at any rate. Those Italian and German soldiers are paid, you know. Professional.

What. What are—

They have all kinds of skills. I'll scratch your back, you scratch mine. So I've heard.

The insult is outrageous but María says nothing. Focuses more intently on her hand. Julita continues talking, mostly to herself. Let her drown in her own bile. So much for electricity. All she can think of is his eyesight worsening from the strain of darkness. He conserves the candles under the stairs. Already they are not easy to come by. If he is suffering, he doesn't complain. His smile flickers in the candlelight, full of kindness and appreciation. But when they lie in the dark, she senses his despair.

~~Respectable, affectionate lady, widowed, home-maker, of modest income would like to meet tall, mild-mannered widower (40 to 45 years) for serious relationship.~~

~~Respectable widow of some means would like to meet serious gentleman (aged 40 to 45) (no divorcees), with a view to marriage.~~

~~Attractive, presentable, hard-working widow (teenage son still at home) seeks widower (40 to 45 yrs) of reasonable means for serious relationship.~~

~~Attractive, respectable widow seeks gentleman, bachelor or widower, of reasonab~~

~~Hard-working widow with teenage son~~

~~Attractive, hard-working widow with teenage son would like to meet gentleman~~

~~Attractive, hard-working widow, of modest means, with teenage son, would like to meet gentleman of similar disposition with a view to marriage.~~

Attractive, hard-working widow of modest means, with teenage son, would like to meet gentleman (40 to 45 yrs) of similar disposition with a view to marriage.

Reason goes out the window on all sides. Unthinkable things become the norm, such as the whirr of mortar shells outside the house. Children under the table, habit now, expecting the rumble, shattered glass. Hands over ears. The impact, sometimes close by, sometimes far. A few seconds in case the house falls down, and out they crawl to resume their game, their book, their chores. Without a word, which is not to say no one is trembling. Is this a good thing. To become used to war and its demands.

Encarna brings eggs. Not at all, she says. Who else would I share them with. Since Joselito died you are my family, you know that. She pats María's arm. Anyway, Tomás needs to grow tall and strong so he can help me run the bar. Tomás always smiles at that. You will take care of the hens if anything happens to me, she says, won't you.

Three eggs. Why would there be more. One for Alicia, one for Tomás, one for María. At dinner, the children stare at their mother's egg. Uneaten. It could be an artefact in a museum. They stare at her strange excuses. Not hungry, the strangest of them all. More plausible, she's keeping the egg to barter for something else tomorrow, *turrón* for Christmas, perhaps. Only one week to go and they smile. Treats, at least, make sense.

That's not all Encarna brought. There is news of the Republican troops still holding their position around the town. She didn't need to elaborate. Artillery fire all afternoon kept everyone on edge. They know what shelling can do to a building. And in case they forget, Julita indulges in stories of schools and hospitals bombed by the fascists in Madrid.

She talks so much, María grumbles as she passes the stairs.

Pressing close to him in his box, much later, she takes the boiled egg out of her pocket. Only half each but the pleasure is shared. Slowly. A delicate hint of days past when they never realised how precious it is to bite into food. A small thing. Its solid texture. Dreamy yellow taste. No one knows what heaven really is.

I love you, he whispers in her ear.

Shh…

The pews are empty. The aisles are empty. The candleholders are empty. The confessionals are empty. The choir is empty. The sacristy is empty. The promises and prayers are empty.

Is there any point.

But for two days now the sky is empty too. Empty of planes. Finally. Empty of noise and dread.

Instead, it fills with flurries. Blizzards. Snow exploding everywhere. Thick white snow. Blessed silent snow. Wildly scattering. Silent targets buried in the blinding snow. Blessed thick white thick, dense and denser blinding. Empty, empty white.

The density of blindness everywhere.

we adapt—we think we need what we're used to—light—movement—space—a certain amount of food

more than in the trench in this box I learn what we can live without—what we can't—for survival at its most basic—but is survival enough—animal underground burrowing deeper into myself

without María it means nothing

death—death of what makes us human

knowing I can be with her—however briefly—I can withstand the cold—the dark—the scarcity of food—the voices and the terror in my head

endure another day just to feel her close at night

is this real

Another letter plagues her through the day. It goes with the others, unanswered, into the top drawer.

Sleep is difficult, of course. Men cry. Call for loved ones 'in their weaker moments', you say. The foreign ones stick together, find comfort in commonality. You take every hardship like a man, waving off their attempts at succour when you were grazed in the arm. I think you tell me this so I'll think highly of you.

Your letters make me sad. Not for the usual reasons. I get sad thinking of what, or who, stripped you of yourself. Who, or what, hollowed out the place where love should be and replaced it with bombs and boots and blades. I get sad remembering all the ways I tried to ask you these things and all the ways you avoided answering.

lying in the ditch—endless nights of crawling—endless days

shaded under trees in the noonday heat—elbows raw—bleeding knees and feet

in noon shade under endless trees—lying in my blood—the endless heat—raw nights—ditch of elbows—knees

thump—beside me a bull fallen from the tree I hadn't seen

was he dead—a bull can't fall from a tree

flayed elbows—stinging eyes—tricks of the mind—can a bull really fall from a tree

the shock distracted me from the agony of open sores—the bull no bull—a man now endless at my feet

a man fallen from a tree—not a bull

had he been lying on a branch—asleep—hiding—deserter perhaps

still warm but dead—from the fall or the murderous heat or something else—a militiaman no doubt on the run—like me

rifle—cartridges—two cigarettes—pocketed

water in his flask—warm but water nevertheless

I squeezed and shook that flask and shook some more for every last drop

Staying indoors is essential for survival but not as easy as it might seem. Time expands and the world shrinks to the size of the house. With nothing to do, nowhere to go, the mind embarks on its own adventures. Already it is crossing deserts from the east, where bright stars dot the sky. As many stars as snowflakes here.

One week to Christmas, twigs are transformed into kings of Orient, labouring towards a pregnant woman, an elderly man, random shepherds. Pebbles become ox and ass. The children have shared their efforts with Encarna in exchange for remnants of fabric to dress their characters. She loves María's children as if they were her own, but it's more than that. Soldiers at the bar have been speaking of plans to offer safe passage out of town for civilians. Soon. In some ways, it's a difficult decision, but on the other hand... She will talk to their mother.

They return home laden with Encarna's embroidered pillowcases for costumes, Bohemian crystal glasses for candles, a vial for imaginary frankincense, a filigree dish from Córdoba for royal gold, two mirrors for special effects, a metal jewellery box on metalwork legs with red velvet interior for something called myrrh that not even Encarna is sure will fit in such a box, because no one has ever seen myrrh before.

Noooo! the children whine when their mother asks them to take the treasures back. She can't bear to think why Encarna is giving them away. Bouncing in the kitchen, excited, oblivious to what the gifts mean, the children explain. It's very important. For the Christmas play. But it's a secret. That's all they can say. Encarna is sworn to secrecy, so there's no point in asking her. Patience, they tell María, and all will be revealed.

discomfort and pain again—over and over and minutely analysed

shoulders—they can be moved in silence—rolled up and back and around

still pain persists—if only I had a cigarette

the hollow where my rifle sat—recoil—recoil—recoil

and the noise—hearing it here under the stairs—here in my head—in every small knock on the other side of the wall

my whole body flinches—if only I could deny this body—disown it—be someone else

think of her—think of her face—her eyes—black—the way she looks at me—beautiful sweet María

conjure her lips—odalisque—and her taste—the honey sweet

think her—want her—think the feel—the soft—the wet—think her thighs

recoil—the hole—the blood—no

think—think her dark—her fingers slim around me—think the soft—her mouth—her tongue—the bullet—no—think—think her breasts—her inside her—María María—faster think—faster think—trigger—no—María—think her soft—his guts—his— fuck—NO—María think—please—María please—his hole—his head—her face—her please—please—please—María—please

Saturday evening and Julita is busy cheating between her running commentary on everything. Running objections and complaints. Manolo, beside her, holds his cards close. For reasons no one has ever spoken about, no one draws attention to her cheating. Manolo looks at María to see if she has noticed his mother's move. María smiles, as if there is nothing amiss, surprised at how easy it is.

Do you think that husband of yours might have got sense and switched allegiance, Julita asks. Those Francoist bullies have no chance. They're mistaken if they think God is on their side. Or maybe he deserted. María tenses. You'd have heard from him otherwise.

Nails painted crimson this evening. Where is she getting a permanent supply of nail varnish. Do her nails never chip on her way to the Communist building.

Apparently they're properly starving now, Julita continues. They'll never win Madrid. Fernando said so in his letter the other day. He says our forces are far superior. Besides, what will they do to Spain if they win. Don't you think men and women should be treated equally.

The dim light is kind to her, María thinks, careful not to rise to her sister's provocation. Too much light on things destroys them. Chiaroscuro, the old painters called it. Brighter when contrasted with the dark.

Encarna breaks the silence to say something about Ramón. He is a good man. Is that what she is saying. It doesn't matter. Julita is in full flow, outsaying whatever it is.

María thinks of him while her sister thrusts barbs and Encarna tries to offer wisdom. He is watching—at the very least listening—because he can do nothing else. In some ways, it's a comfort to know he is there. To know she can confide in him later, tell him about the letters, her fears.

Past the seminary, dots of light on the hillside. Nationalist troops, she tells him. They've surrounded the town to help the Nationalists that are still holding out at the Seminary.

He nods, knowing the resilience of the military and their superior weaponry. He remembers Toledo and how they held the fortress. Utter destruction. It was hard to imagine anyone inside could have survived. But they did.

The Republicans are setting up barricades at the cemetery and Plaza del Torico, she continues. They're determined to gain control of the town. I expect it will be vicious, she frowns. The roads and railway line are blocked. No one can get in or out.

I thought they were going to let... he begins, but she tightens her grip on his arm to silence him.

The government opened all routes for civilians this morning. Between 7 a.m. and 9 a.m. Her face is starting to crumple in anguish. They have spoken about this before. He feels her muscles tense with distress.

So... Encarna...

All María can do is nod. Death is bad enough. But to have to grieve for the living.

Did she say when she'll be back.

There is no answer. They hold each other, to restore some balance to their lives. Honeyed in this light, neither of them cares how much time passes, who might be looking for María on the other side of the wall. Here they are safe, though the meaning of safe is also changing with the war. They have each other, at least, when so much unwanted circumstance is foisted on them and must somehow be incorporated into every day.

He tells her about the disillusion so many of his comrades felt. He has told her before. The betrayal by their own side is hard to understand. They should be rallying together—for democracy if nothing else, for basic rights of working men and women—instead of splintering. He takes a deep breath. They are all too hungry for power, he scoffs. I hope the rebels run the Republicans out of town. The Republicans will destroy Spain. I see it now. They've already destroyed it.

Stillness descends under the stairs. Talk of destruction and betrayal feels almost like a prelude to the real question. Who are they really betraying. Themselves. The others.

she couldn't

what's she looking at—surely she can't hear my breathing—my heart thumping

why is it that when we most need to be silent we most want to clear our throat

such a penetrating stare it's as if she can see through the wall—no

she couldn't

More than any ideal, uncertainty unites everyone who is walking to the outskirts of town. They don't look back because the exodus is only going one way. Left behind are people too old or infirm to walk. What will happen to them, María wonders. Unplanned, a line forms. Ragged. One after the other, carts, children, hens and goats. They have somewhere to go, don't they. They must have relatives somewhere else. What few houses remain intact are practically empty by now.

You and the children must come with me, María, Encarna implores, holding on to the very end. You know I love you like a daughter. My brother will welcome you.

What must she think of her feeble excuse. In case Ramón returns. She can't tell her the truth, although she has been tempted to so many times.

Ramón will find you. You're being unreasonable, my dear. Think of the children.

I prefer to stay, Encarna. Just in case.

In case what. What is it, María... Encarna pleads. Anything to explain this inexplicable stubbornness. María, always so reasonable. What can have possessed her.

The only other time she ever saw Encarna look distressed was when Joselito died. But how can she explain the impossible. I prefer to stay, that's all. Come back safely, Encarna.

I don't understand you. Encarna is close to tears. It's dangerous here. You know that. When you get sense, my dear, promise you will come to the farm. Alicia, Tomás, you must do the nativity play without me. Tell me all about it when I come back.

To the children she gives a hen each. A small box into María's hands. Just in case you need it, she says, hugging her tightly.

No, Encarna, please. She knows it contains money, a gesture of finality that is unbearable.

so many of them young boys not much older than Manolo—dear boys

I think of Fernando and José—would they have signed up had they known the smell of futility and rotting bodies

and grown men—how can they condone what their comrades are doing—democracy at what cost—no one could possibly have imagined this

the charred face of that nun against the convent wall comes back to me—frozen in supplication—blackened bones—skin like leather—the terror I felt at being transfixed like that by death— unable to look away

anarchists—they said—the anarchists did that

were we not all in this together—fighting a common enemy

I am a coward—to my shame I am a coward—but the government—what's left of it—has fled the capital to Valencia— Madrid to fend for itself with bare fists—is that not cowardice

is it unpatriotic to think this

the Republic or the rebels—to support one side is to support a hatred of the other—feed it till it eats you up and blinds you— how do we allow ourselves to be so duped

was this to be the basis of agricultural reform

I am a coward who cannot forget that man—el mosca—beaten till his bones were so badly broken his arms and legs could be tied in a bow behind his head—skewered with a pike and trussed like a pig for the spit—how did he not make a sound—just kept blinking—blinking

Shelling causes damage to a house even if the walls don't collapse or catch fire. She looks at the windows criss-crossed with sticky tape. A trick she learnt early on. When Inés was born. Doctor García told her about the terrible injuries that flying glass can cause. The thought of it.

Now this box of money that Encarna gave her. What can money buy with everyone gone and the town in ruins. Might it have been better to give the children the opportunity to get out. The countryside is always safer. Wide spaces. Places to hide.

One of the windows is cracked. A spider's web barely held by the sticky tape. It will only take the slightest rumble. Then the snow will flutter right into the kitchen. Gently mantle them in white.

Money won't fix any of it, she says to the wall.

Because of you, Julita replies.

María stares at her sister. *Because of me.* You didn't leave when you had the chance *because of me.*

Yes, *because of you.* Look at you. You've lost it. Completely lost it. You're not thinking straight. Who in their right mind would keep children in this place. It's ready to fall on top of you if anyone as much as sneezes. And for such a stupid reason.

María is speechless.

Yes, Encarna told me. I never heard such nonsense in all my life. Julita is indignant. This is the last place that husband of yours would start looking for you, if he ever comes back. A bombed-out town. Seriously. You need your head examined. You're not fit to take care of the children in that state of mind. You're overwhelmed, paralysed by everything. You need someone to take care of you, and who'd do that if I left. I can't leave. I wouldn't do such a selfish thing. I've heard you talking to yourself. She pauses, in case María might want to elucidate, but María doesn't. I don't blame you, her sister picks up again. Don't think I do. I know it's hard, María, but some of us are stronger than others, and the stronger ones need to look out for the others. Manolo can sleep in the children's room. I'll take the other room.

You can't, she stutters. There's no... How will we...

Exactly my point, says Julita. You can't see the simple logic of things, and now it's too late to leave. They've blocked the exits to the city again. We're stuck here, I'm afraid. But I'm here now. We'll make the best of it. You can be thankful I'm so involved in the Communist Party. My comrades in town will help us. We help each other, you know, not that you care about that. The windows were all blown out at home with the shelling a few days ago, she adds. We were already dying of the cold before that. It's more practical if we are all here.

Trying to sound in control of herself, she says, Ramón is due back soon.

Julita looks at her sister as if she is looking at an impostor. Sure. She inhales deeply. Manolo, son, will you take your things up to the cousins' room. She starts to gather some of the bags she has brought. Look, she turns to María with a smile, I brought wool.

Clickety clickety click. The most important thing, Julita insists, is that it can end the war. Mystifying, but it has been explained by the militias in town. The Communist building is full of wisdom. Stockings and scarves for the men at the front. One plain. One purl. If they are warmer their morale will improve and the Republic will prevail. Although their morale is good anyway, because they are having many victories as they advance. She has heard it on the radio at the Communist building. The militias all confirm it. If their morale is good they will be in more positive spirits when they fight the rebels. And if, if, if. Plain purl plain purl they will win the war. So the sooner plain purl the better. One of the officers, very attractive, in charge, says a truck will come in two days to collect all donations in time for Christmas.

María watches her sister teach the children to knit. The novelty doesn't last long but the long faces persist at the thought of what they are missing on Encarna's brother's farm. Sulking needles dip and stitches drop but Julita refuses to be defeated. Come on now, sit up straight. It would be unpatriotic not to contribute to the front.

If you're going to stay in my house, at least don't talk about patriotism.

There are Republican troops in Madrid bravely defending the capital, Julita continues, trying to disguise the sharp cadences in her voice. Brave men prepared to give their lives like…like my Antonio, and Fernando and José. The government is encouraging us all to give whatever we can. They deserve it.

You were never one to take orders from anyone, María retorts, but you're happy to take them from—

This is different, her sister says.

This is a disorganised bunch of hooligans who have done nothing but cause mayhem and murder for the past five years. They don't even know what side they're on. There is no government. None to speak of. They are puppets of that fellow in Russia, Julita. And you talk of patriotism. What exactly are they fighting for. What were they ever fighting for. Tell me.

Julita stares at her sister. For better conditions for us. For democracy, she says.

María scoffs. Thousands tortured and killed because they don't agree with you, regardless of who they are, because they don't belong to this version of Communism, of anarchy, or to the fellow in Russia, or Troski or whatever his name is, or that other fellow they have over there. Max.

Clickety click click. I don't know what you're talking about. Honestly, you've lost it. Where did you come up with such far-fetched guff. Who are those people, anyway. We want equal distribution of wealth, María. That's what we want. We want equal pay for women, the right to vote, secular education.

Even if it means killing people who don't agree with you, is that it. Even if it means rigging elections. Is that the democracy you want.

Honestly, you're more gone in the head than I thought.

They have grown-up purpose now and don't care if the rug is damp, moth-ridden.

I found it, Tomás is quick to tell his sister as he drags it with Manolo to their tent amidst the rubble of the barber's shop. An impressive addition. Pulled here, there, this way, that, and finally into the best position.

Strike it, Tomás urges Manolo.

What are you doing, Alicia asks.

Cigarettes, her brother announces with an air of importance. He is eleven, after all. Should we…, he turns to Manolo, nodding towards his sister.

Weighty decisions they don't normally have to make.

Sure, Manolo smiles, and Alicia fills with pride. Here, he offers her a butt.

Don't tell Mamá we let you, Tomás insists, or we'll never bring you with us again.

The flame fizzes blue, turns to yellow, and Manolo brings it to the butt in his mouth. Sucks in. It's not the first time. Alicia and Tomás wait their turn in awe. You try, Manolo says to them, holding out the flame. But it burns. Ouch. New strike.

Tomás first, and instantly the smoke strips the inside of his mouth and throat. Eyes streaming, he coughs, choking, barely able to catch his breath while Manolo doubles over, laughing hard.

Well, do you like it, he asks.

Why is he laughing when her brother's face is green. Alicia is alarmed. More puzzled still when Tomás nods, and yes, he splutters, he likes it.

these nightmares—Juanjo with me on the count's estate at night—
but we never hunted there

dark as under these stairs—uneasy flicker of moonlight through
the trees—we shouldn't be here—whose idea was it—I only hunt
in the forest—why here

he aims and the deer looks up—but it's not a deer—it's me

Juanjo—I want to tell him it's me—I am not a deer—but I am and
I can't speak

I freeze—Juanjo is not Juanjo either—he is and he isn't—he is
Juanjo pointing the rifle at me but he is the count and I have been
found—his finger pulls the trigger and I wake in a sweat in a
dank hole afraid to breathe

did I shout in my sleep

She wakes at the usual time. Dresses. Goes downstairs. It hits her as she whispers good morning to the wall. Encarna is gone and the bar is closed. The kitchen window stares at her, white wall of snow criss-crossed by tape. There is nothing to look at, it mocks. Nowhere to go.

If Julita wasn't up in the bedroom she'd sneak in with him, but she can't take that chance. Julita Julita Julita. At least there are the bags of food she brought with her last night. She cuts two slices of bread, lifts the loose slat, quiet, quiet, quick. Hands them to him with a jug of water, pointing to the upper floor, shaking her head in despair. I love you, he mouths. She remembers something. Replaces the slat, keeping an eye on the top of the stairs, rummages through the second bag and returns. No one will miss it. Quickly, the slat again and his face again, biting his bottom lip in disbelief. He hasn't seen a tomato in months.

Julita's knitting is on the table and María's scream is caught in her throat. Stockings and scarves for the troops. Food parcels for the troops. Christmas treats for the troops. Wine. And what about us, she wants to shout. What about town after town that is falling to the fascists. Is her sister really so gullible. What does she think the Republican troops are doing here if not diverting Franco's men from their progress towards Madrid. There is no other reason. This is not a town worth taking. It's a nothing. A backwater on the way to nowhere. We are nothing but pawns, she thinks. We have nothing to eat—chicken bones for broth if we're lucky and a few miserable berries. The birds have a better diet. What is the Republic doing about that.

everything magnifies through this hole as if it were a microscope

your back to me gently swaying as you stir the pot—a pot of steam

every inch of your body—I go through it to stop going mad

how will we survive now that the bar has closed and the town emptied—now that Julita is here

the night is the worst—the silence—endless hours—afraid I'll snore or make some noise in my sleep

how can I be sure I am silent in this box—outside they have their ways of ensuring silence

in here is permanent night were it not for the sounds of the kitchen

in my head a permanent roar and I don't know how to make it stop

She takes a deep breath. Burning her fingers, another letter. A world of difference between these and the letters her mother used to receive. They were fresh air every time they arrived. Sisters back in Seville sending sunshine to Aragón. Weekly missives, fat and packed with excitement. Children growing. Lumbago. The price of chard. Marriages. Local fiestas. New recipes. The envelopes promised love and never disappointed, whatever news they imparted. She thinks of her mother waiting for quiet before sitting down to savour the words. An indulgence like few others. Far from the torment of these letters. Sometimes she considers not reading them at all.

A rust coloured smudge on the page. Maybe it's not yours. Your hand is as neat and well formed as if you were sitting comfortably at a proper desk. Your mind as sharp.

Distance is good. I see you more clearly. I can think of you without the pain. I now know pain comes from expectation. But why should we not expect. Why should a woman obliterate herself at the service of others. And why do we teach this to our daughters.

You were so beautiful when we first met. I would have given you anything. I wanted to give you everything. My body, my mind, my life. I would have loved you like no one else. But you couldn't see that. Love means something different to you. Something more practical. Closer to service. Servitude. I understand that now, now that you're not here, but do you know the emptiness that leaves in my heart.

Uribe's brains—pink—Uribe's brains—black—Uribe's brains—
red—Uribe's brains—green—Uribe's brains—grey—Uribe's
brains—purple —Uribe's brains—yellow—Uribe's brains—
blue—Uribe's brains—brown

what colour are Uribe's brains

pink—WRONG—what colour are Uribe's brains

black—WRONG—what colour are Uribe's brains

red—WRONG—what colour are Uribe's brains

green—WRONG—what colour are Uribe's brains

grey—WRONG—what colour are Uribe's brains

purple—WRONG—what colour are Uribe's brains

yellow—WRONG—what colour are Uribe's brains

blue—WRONG—what colour are Uribe's brains

brown—WRONG—what colour are Uribe's brains

what colour—what colour—what colour—WRONG

pink—black—red—green—WRONG—grey—purple—yellow—
WRONG—blue—brown—WRONG

idiot

IDIOT

URIBE HAS NO BRAINS

Uribe's brains are stuck to the soles of your boots and the side of your face

Julita's moods make the house smaller and smaller. Moods like enemy fire. Will it come. Will it not. When, then. Not this morning. This morning there is a truce. Julita and the children are gone, snow or no snow, shell fire or not. Stockings need to be delivered to the Communist building.

In the stillness of the empty house they have one hour like normal people. Upstairs. Moments stolen from the war. From life itself. Moments when they can be exactly who they want to be. As if nothing else in the world mattered and he didn't have to hide.

Living in a box does strange things to a man. He has lost strength and even the dim light is too glaring. He seems frightened of the light. Frightened of the creaking stove pipe. Frightened of the softness of the bed.

His eyes half closed for longer than she recalls before they adjust. Bones ache when he stretches, ache when he moves. Almond milk his skin, pale, but warm against the treachery of winter. And his voice that she rarely hears properly anymore, it too is weaker from whispering but mellow still, and deep.

How did this happen, they keep wondering, and neither of them really knows whether they mean the war or this impossible love they are living. Two extremes and neither makes sense. Less sense, the happiness they feel. In the midst of destruction, of terror, this tenderness that should not exist. We are like those insects that live in the dark, he muses. The ones that survive underground, unseen, when the larger creatures are wiped out. The blind ones who feel nothing.

She stares at him. I don't understand.

I love you. But what does that mean if I am invisible, dead to the world, in that box.

But you are not, she thinks, invisible or dead to me. I couldn't keep going without you, she says. We will be together when the war ends. Together like now. We will make it possible, my love. It will happen. She cups his face in her hands. Strokes his cheek.

He smiles at her and says yes, they will be together, but in his head he thinks the war will never end. How can this thing that began so long ago and has infiltrated them to their core ever be completely purged. The war will always be part of who they are and they will never be able to make it end. We are the war, he thinks. We will always be the war. Dragged into it. Deformed by it. Reduced to animals by it.

You're right, he says, because he wants to make her smile again. He needs to see her smile. When the war ends we will be together. The way we were before.

Flour. Vegetables. Meat would be such a treat. Is it madness to dream.

Where are you going like that, Julita snaps. You'll catch your death of cold.

María stops in her tracks. Inhales. I don't have anything warmer. Do you think I like going out like this. But someone has to try and get food.

You're hopeless, Julita shakes her head. Hold on a minute.

Stockings. Sweater. Scarf.

What else have you stashed in your room.

Oh, the troops won't miss one or two items. She brushes the idea aside and María stares. Her sister who always has everything under control, who needs people and things to take charge of and boss about. Her words from the other evening come back, when they were playing cards. Who is scratching whose back, she wonders. And how.

Manolo, go with aunty. She'll need help with the bags.

It takes over an hour to make the journey that would ordinarily take fifteen minutes. The city is unrecognisable. A mountain of rubble buried under snow. They set out for the square on the strength of nothing but hope. For weeks it has been almost not worth queuing for the butcher because the streets are impassable. And the roads into town. Few supplies are getting in. But Christmas. The children haven't had meat in weeks.

Turrón, Julita said, and I will have marzipan too. Without explanation. Pilfered, perhaps, from the parcels for the troops. María doesn't dare suggest such a thing. She's in no position to hold moral ground.

The viaduct is still standing, heavy military presence around it. Soldiers who are most of them not really soldiers. Militiamen. Rifles from behind every barricade made of debris are what give them soldierly status, but their overall demeanour is dishevelled. They stand at their post and it's plain they're not sure what they should be doing. Much of the time there is nothing to do except beat their hands for warmth, smoke, chat to pretty girls. The few that are left in town. As María and Manolo approach, the men straighten up and look officious.

Hold my hand, she urges, hoping it will make him look younger.

In the queue outside the butcher there is praise for the militias. They are referred to as soldiers. They have held their ground, defeated Franco's rebels. It was on the radio this morning, now on everyone's lips. The Nationalists have been defeated by our brave soldiers. But there is no fanfare. How is that. No meat either.

She repeats everything she heard as soon as she gets home, close to the wall. The cavalry are pushing back the Nationalists, she relays.

Does Papá have a horse, the children want to know.

He does, a beautiful white horse.

A big horse, they ask.

Yes, of course. A big white horse like El Cid, and they run off pretending to be heroes on horseback. *Viva España*, they cry, galloping onto the battlefield.

She looks at them, their energy. Thinks of the men at the front, fighting. But fighting won't fix broken lives. It will be the children who will have to do that.

I'm going out of my mind

I'm going out of my mind

I'm going out of my mind

think of something else

exercise

step forward—watch your head

step back—watch your back

step right—small step—mind the wall

step left—small step—mind the wall

step forward—mind your head

step back—mind your back

to the right—the wall

to the left—the wall

pretend it's the countryside—the sky—blue—clouds—trees—
leaves and their veins and the light shimmering through—
dappled light—waves of colour—ouch

mind your head

There is grit in the snow because Alicia doesn't discriminate between the clean surface snow and the snow lying directly on the ground. As a result, Tomás is upset and throws the bucket of dirty snow at the door. So much care and effort gone to waste.

She's a baby, he grumbles, red faced. To stanch the tears, he stomps up the stairs, putting special emphasis on each word. A useless, good-for-nothing baby.

Perfect trigger for Julita. An avalanche of complaints about rudeness, wild behaviour, possible damage to the door, her sister's lack of control over her children.

Don't worry, son, everything has a solution. We can boil the snow and pass it through a muslin cloth so the grit gets left behind.

During Julita's tirade about extra efforts required thanks to Alicia's stupidity, about muslin being needed for other things, about lack of proper discipline, María remains calm. She smiles at Tomás, willing him to drown out Julita's drill. Listen, son, if we use the muslin we will have crystal clear water. It's simple. You've done good work. Even Alicia's snow can be used. Come on, bring the bucket inside.

The angst in his face relaxes at this possibility. Conciliatory, he comes down the stairs. For María, it is a minor triumph.

It only takes minutes. See, she later says with a smile, we now have clean water.

The razor blades are worn again. She makes light of his wild, unkempt look, but underneath the frivolity they know the most basic of civilities are being eroded the longer he stays hidden under the stairs.

Yesterday his beard represented utter defeat. Shh... I will get you more, she whispered, thinking of packed ice, the pitiless hole that used to be the barber's shop, and all the things he needs being donated to the front—shaving soap, fancy safety razors, gloves, socks.

She will go to the barber's house instead. If he didn't leave town. Ask for two blades, even the old kind will do, and say they are a gift for Manolo who will surely need them soon. Ramón was a good customer. Goodwill is due. A gift for the boy to make him feel like a man even though his skin is still as smooth as the day he was born.

The question of why José, her eldest, hasn't written in months has been gnawing at Julita. Fernando's letters arrive, envelopes visibly tampered with, but full of good cheer and optimism about their efforts. Maybe in the Eastern Front, where Fernando is, the mail is quicker than on the Guadarrama Front. Mail is erratic these days, the postman assures her. Maybe José has less time to write because fighting is more intense around the capital. Or maybe... Other reasons she doesn't want to contemplate settled months ago in the pit of her stomach. She writes every week, regardless.

Her heart has been thumping wildly since his letter arrived but she has waited for the right moment. Just in case. Although if anything had happened, the letter would be from the government. Wouldn't it. Official stamp. Drowned.

On the bed now, afraid to open the letter, she stalls, props two pillows behind her. Unconscious need for comfort. What kind of world would it be if no one ever sent letters. She slashes along the edge that has not been properly resealed.

Relief. Not bad news but it's worrying. Confusing. He thanks her for writing last month but asks why she hasn't replied to his many letters. What letters. She hasn't received any. He says he is well, alive at least, walking now without his toes. Because his letters have gone unanswered and things continue the same as ever, he simply sends love. Lots of hugs and kisses. P.S. I really need those boots. And socks, the thicker the better. P.P.S. Tell

Manolito I've got good at arm wrestling. He won't win so easily next time.

Mostly, the letter contains a troubled silence that drops onto her lap.

the loose plank on the stairs lifts

I hold my breath every time—as if I were underwater

hold while you descend

hold your foot ankle knee thigh

hold buttocks hips waist

hold stomach torso breasts shoulders

hold neck arms elbows wrists hands

hold the wooden slat replaced

breathe

LA VANGUARDIA

Barcelona	DAILY AT THE SERVICE OF DEMOCRACY	15 cents
Year LVI. – No. 23,020	Offices: Pelayo 28 Telephone: 14135	Thursday 23 December, 1937

Republican Flags in Teruel

EDITORIAL

Consequences of Victory

The first consequence of this victory for the Republican Army has been to justify Mr Attlee's campaign in England. As our readers know, and will not forget despite the recent and important events in Teruel, that the British Labour leader, leader of the opposition in the House of Commons, came to Spain and saw our cities – Barcelona, Valencia, Madrid – and visited the fronts. Upon returning to his country, he proclaimed the unquestionable truths he had ascertained, one of which–of most interest to us at this present moment–was that the strength, organisation and efficiency of the Army created by the Republic, from scant resources and against the most stringent odds, was truly marvellous and would not be long in achieving surprising results. Thanks to the victory in Teruel, Mr. Attlee's words have acquired a significance that will give the most sceptical and conservative Englishmen pause for thought.

Mr. Attlee and his noble defence of Spain have frequently been in our thoughts during these jubilant days, and some of our celebration is dedicated to him.

The repercussions of this victory will extend to other countries. The Fascists approached, insolently bragging about their plans of an offensive, alleging it would be ruthless in conception and execution, based on their successes in the Northern Front, which are not successes in military terms, and on the weakness of the Republic...

Is something wrong, María asks.

No, nothing. Just a letter from José. It seems I haven't got any of the letters he's been sending.

The children look up. José, Manolo exclaims. What does he say.

A watery smile from his mother. Oh, nothing much. He is well, missing us. And he's going to beat you at arm wrestling when he comes back.

Manolo beams. Ha, never.

It seems to give his mother confidence. Does that husband of yours not write, do we know if he's dead or alive at least. Maybe he's in hospital.

María smarts. Her sister never lets anything upset her for long. Not when she has someone to lash out at. I'd have heard if he was in hospital. You can't expect him to spend his time writing in the middle of a battlefield, she says.

Rubbish. They all write. He'll have to come home soon, anyhow, with the war nearly won.

The war is far from over, Julita.

My God, you're such a killjoy. It's on the radio every day at the Communist building, my dear. The Republican positions are intact and steadily gaining ground. That's what they're saying.

You believe whatever you want, María retorts. Who is saying these things.

The General Workers' Union has called on everyone in Barcelona to come out to the streets tomorrow and celebrate. The glorious victory of our troops, they called it. I heard it this morning. Maybe there'll be something here to mark the occasion.

With the rubble and rotting bodies in the streets, and the snowdrifts, I doubt it.

There you go again. She sighs. I'm going to the Communist building. I may not be back till late.

On the thin mattress with their backs to the wall, he draws her even closer. Her sadness in the candlelight has a particular serenity. I really wish I could have been here when Inés died. He takes a breath. I haven't said it before because I didn't want to upset you, but it pains me to think you had to go through that on your own.

She squeezes his arm with a smile. There was nothing you could have done. To be honest, the one who let me down was Julita. She knew the difficulty I was having, how tired I was, the milk drying up. And she did nothing.

She has always been jealous of you. Jealous of everyone. She wanted a daughter but… They're very fine lads, the three of them. But she's never satisfied with anything.

María nods in the silence, each caught in a labyrinth of possibilities. Ifs and buts until a justification can be found.

She was always mean to you, María says, bossing you around, belittling you in front of everyone. I don't know how you held your tongue. She doesn't tell him how she cringed at her sister's constant put-downs. Watching him pass it off as if it were nothing felt like a physical assault to her.

To keep the peace, he smirks. You and I are very alike in that regard. We put up with things.

Cheering in the streets. Music from an open window hovers over the small crowd. Then firecrackers. Among the revellers she sees doctor García. His smile is cautious, observant more than jubilant.

Doctor, she waves. It's official then, she calls, unsure herself of whether it is a statement or a question. The Republicans have defeated Franco's troops.

I hope it's true, he says, lumbering up to her. You'd think all of Spain had been won but every other city has fallen to the rebels. I'm afraid very little has been won so far.

She thinks of him alone under the stairs this afternoon. I hope the military run the Republicans out of town, he said some days ago while they lay together late into the night. The Republicans will ruin Spain. They already have. If they win this war it will just be more of the same. Their endless political disagreements. Socialists against Communists, or Workers Parties against Anarchists, or some combination of these against some combination of the other. They seem incapable of pulling together to get anything done.

My apologies, señora Vázquez, the doctor says, noticing her sadness. I am thinking of my patients. Some are living in derelict buildings. Illness is not their enemy. They will die of the cold and hunger before the week is out. But of course this is a moment to celebrate. My God, he points behind her.

Is Julita dancing with a stranger. A soldier. Her cheeks are flushed. A firecracker shoots into the clouds. Low hanging, firecracker lost, but the cheers are loud. Julita's head flings back, now carmine lips laughing with the stranger. When was the last time she laughed.

That's my sister, María clarifies. I'm afraid the celebrations have gone to her head.

But the doctor is pointing at something else. Trucks. Out of nowhere. The excitement intensifies. Louder, more heartfelt cries and the word *coal* thickens the air. The celebration gathers pace. Coal. Miraculously. QUICK, a bag of coal. Two. Grab. Push. Men shove, shout, and she is suddenly part of the melee and doesn't care, elbowing people out of the way. What happened to civility.

They carry, drag, pull, roll sacks home, exultant despite the exertion over mounds of rubble. She and the children. Julita with the stranger. Who is he. Who cares. There will be a blazing fire for Christmas.

LA VANGUARDIA

Barcelona   **DAILY AT THE SERVICE OF DEMOCRACY**   **15 cents**

Year LVI. – No. 23,021   Offices: Pelayo 28 Telephone: 14135   Friday 24 December, 1937

Cleanup Operation after Internal Fighting Forges Ahead Uninterrupted in Teruel

Last three Strongholds Defending Teruel Fall to Popular Army

From the early hours of this morning, the task of penetrating Teruel has continued, giving us an insight into the lack of culture and sheer insanity in the Fascist camp. Two fifteen-year-old youths, leaders of the Falange in charge of action groups and cleanup operations, have been captured. Terrified by the imminent prospect of popular justice, that will be equitable in punishing their crimes and insanity, and by the insistent and constant barrage of our artillery and cannons, the two minors willingly, albeit trembling, came to us and handed over their weapons.

Our soldiers are making steady and speedy progress through the city streets and houses... On occasion, our men have caught Fascists by the scruff of the neck as they were in the act of firing through a window. Plaza del Torico has been decisively taken. Two houses in the square, used as strongholds, are now ours. We have also taken the Town Hall and one of the handful of Civil Guard barracks that had been in enemy hands.

On the outskirts, our soldiers have gathered many corpses. The cleanup operation inside the city is almost complete. Nothing is left of the enemy resistance.

it's hard not to believe the lies—they've done it with every battle since this began—spreading news of victory well before the battle is over

it's too soon to admit defeat but this is a defeat—what have they won so far—what city has been successfully taken—what policy have they implemented that worked

I never thought a single life could be dispensable—I knew nothing of bodies left rotting in the heat because they are fodder—hundreds of them—and the stench—maggots as sickening as our government the way it's going about this business—change yes—but it has to be feasible—for everyone's benefit—good men can't just be the pawns in a sophisticated project—a political game—Brunete forever a nightmare—every night—and in my waking hours too—I will never escape

the officers were just following orders—it's the government I can never forgive—what they put us through—no foliage for camouflage—ferocious heat—hellfire thirst

pebbles saved me some days—they keep the saliva coming in the mouth—but we were sitting ducks—it's hard not to be bitter—they could have stopped the slaughter but they were too proud to admit defeat

instead they kept spreading lies—sending out more and more men—fodder—me victory within our grasp they'd say—this town won—rebels repelled—none of it true and still they spread the same lies and still they are believed and I am here

Christmas Eve and Julita has disappeared with Manolo. There's the meal to be prepared for tonight, though how festive it can be with nothing in the larder weighs on María's mind. Encarna always brought treats.

Lack of food, lack of news about her neighbour. María sits at the table, bare wood, and shivers. She thinks of Inés. Considers crying but hasn't the energy. Instead her grievances are for the wall. Were her sister not likely to come back at any moment she would climb in with him.

How long. One hour. Two. The children have been busy rehearsing the nativity scene. Remember, Mamá, how we used Inesita as the baby in the manger last year. Can she see us from heaven, Mamá. They ask as if they were asking the time of day.

Of course she can, María smiles.

Will Encarna be here.

No, pet. I don't know. Rehearse, just in case.

When is Manolo coming back. We need Manolo. He's a shepherd.

He'll be here soon. He just went out for a few minutes with his mother.

Soon slides into noon. Manolo bursts in the door and she can't remember the last time he looked as happy. Baskets. His mother behind him with more baskets. Eggs, salami, bread, olives, two rabbits, *turrón*.

I thought we'd never make it back, Julita huffs, lifting their hoard onto the table. I was scared we'd be stopped by the Popular Army. There are troops milling in the streets after their victory. I thought if they stopped us and saw what we had they'd take it from us, even though everyone is saying the streets are safer now and even cleaner, with the debris being removed. They're hungry, poor men.

Where did you get all this. She is thinking of the stranger Julita was dancing with in the square but Julita dismisses the question. Have you not set the table yet. What have you been doing all morning, she asks, taking one item after another out of the baskets. For God's sake, you're hopeless. Light the oven, it's Christmas Eve, we have rabbits to roast. Alicia, boil some water. The small pot and for God's sake don't spill it. Your mother is hopeless. Tomás, cut up the *turrón*. Put it on the good platter, not that one.

Bossing, as usual, but who would have thought her orders could be welcome. How everything is to be prepared, how the table is to be set. María's contribution is meagre by comparison— potatoes and the remains of Ramón's sherry. Julita looks at the bottle. But, she begins, what will he say when he comes back.

So often she has goaded her with the idea that he's not coming back.

Well, I suppose he won't miss a little bit, Julita gives in. It's Christmas. Do you remember the Christmas after Antonio and I were married and his uncle gave us a bottle of sweet sherry. My God, it was delicious. You could drink it like lemonade. She laughs at the memory. I thought I only had a small amount, but when I stood up from the table to make the coffee I fell right over, on top of Ramón. Do you remember that. Antonio was mortified. His wife drunk in front of his parents. Even though I was only a tiny bit tipsy. And Antonio's mother made that comment about falling over running in our family because you had that bruise from falling in the bedroom. Poker faced she was. And I couldn't stop laughing until Ramón helped me up, always the gentleman, and helped me to the kitchen to make the coffee. Do you remember.

The candle has burned down to the wick and his hand strokes the soft skin on her thigh, oblivious to the coldest winter on record.

When did she take over, María whispers.

The day she was born. They stifle a laugh. You have my sympathy, he smiles, drawing her closer. Still, rabbit, *turrón*, sherry… I'm not complaining. It probably has something to do with that man you told me she was dancing with. As long as she doesn't bring him here. It was clever of you to ply her with the last of the sherry. She'll sleep soundly.

Her lips are soft. Always welcoming. It feels like a very long time, she says.

Light years. Your smile is beautiful, do you know that. It keeps me alive when I… I watched you all day, weaving lightly among everyone, just in the right place to offer help when it was needed. You are the glue that keeps the household together. Julita thinks she's in charge, but she isn't really. She'd be nothing if she didn't have someone to boss about.

In the stillness, María is mindful of his touch, light, loving, and the perception of his observations. I love you, she kisses him again.

You give quietly, he continues, letting them all take whatever they need. You give just by being there, by making life possible for them, making it possible for her to order you about, for the children to flourish regardless of the hardships.

It's funny how we can have nothing yet have everything, she says. How you understand me sometimes better than I understand myself. That, too, means so much to me.

maps

at least in this box the map is clear—curled in the corner I remember the night I couldn't move—curled in the trench—everything that went wrong

if only we had been given maps—that minimum—we would not have gone belly-crawling blindly to the wrong side of the embankment—whistle of bullets—Uribe's brains—retch even now—wanting to bring him back but couldn't

and Santos—smiley Santos and his cigarettes—alive as we dragged him back—innards spilling out faster than we could push them in—dead by the time we reached the trench—but we tried—we did try

shaking—crumpled in a corner—uncontrollable for who knows how long

maps—so simple—logical—instead I map perpetual darkness—feel its deepest recesses with my fingers—splintered corners—rough joints and the bare brick of the wall

how much longer

Doctor García, frozen at the door. Unsmiling, he sheds his doctorness. Always a humble man. Everything is complicated. Everyone needs something, the impossible. Such a gentle face. What has he seen these past weeks.

Julita is all smiles. Fishing.

No, he replies, addressing María too. I am needed here. I can't leave.

He speaks of shelling, broken windows, ceiling caved in. Asking for her help without asking. The more he describes what's left of his house, the fainter she feels. The kitchen is moving. She leans against the wall and her heart slips through the cracks, under the stairs. A shell of a house, the doctor tells them. Dangerous. She can sense what's coming and her throat constricts. Julita is full of concern. Most of the people left are those who are too old or ill to leave. He cannot impose on them and he cannot abandon them either. There's no room for him at the makeshift hospital.

Stricken, she contains herself. She has no choice. Of course you can stay here, Doctor, she manages without a smile. The back room will be comfortable for you. The children will go with you and help to bring your things. It's safe enough with the fighting at a standstill.

Blizzards have their unexpected advantages, he says. I cannot thank you enough, señora Vázquez.

It will be good to have the doctor stay. Julita's cheerful

interruptions are grating. We must pool together. Those few of us left.

Why is her sister everywhere, upstairs, downstairs, inside her head. Worse than shells. Leave me alone, will you. Just… Just…

Whatever is wrong with you. My God, you're impossible. I'm going with the doctor and the children to help bring his things. You should come too, María. Make yourself useful for a change.

They leave and the house falls silent, perhaps for the last time in a long time. It's too much. I CAN'T BELIEVE THIS, to the wall. I CAN'T BELIEVE IT.

Sometimes it's hard to get through the day. Hard to explain why.

Forcing a smile helps. For the children's sake. The doctor's sake.

Appearances. They can be important. A semblance of the person she once was. Until she's alone again. Upstairs. The baby's cardigans soft and comforting. The room calm, despite the letters.

The doctor is not the imposition she expected. Quite the contrary. He is helpful, discreetly stays out of the way when he's in the house, out most of the time. But this evening, he's not really suggesting...

Again, Julita fusses and flaps around the doctor. Why does she always have to interfere. Of course señora Rojas must come. Whoever you think needs refuge, Doctor. There'll be no more discussion about it, isn't that right, she turns to María. Consider it done, Doctor. We will shelter whoever we can. Gladly.

Most kind, but it is María he fixes with his questioning look and the explanation of why his patient needs refuge. Gentle, his tone. Controlled, though there is no hiding the urgency of the request. Snowflake soft the words blanket her. A strength in the way he sees the solution, in the way he acknowledges this house as hers, and even Julita has stopped talking. Maybe he is a magician. They were in the past. Alchemists, her grandfather told her, with their spells and potions. Blaise with his powers. Could she confide in the doctor, perhaps. He seems to understand things, handle them in a quiet kind of way. Her heart is thumping fast. He expects her to say yes.

I don't know.

What do you mean, you don't know. Julita is indignant. Of course we will take care of your patients, Doctor.

Again his warm smile. How does he manage to acknowledge Julita while ignoring her at the same time.

I understand it is a lot to ask. Please take time to think about it, señora Vázquez.

María, please. Call me María.

You will be helping to save people's lives.

cancelled by circumstance—a spectator of life through a hole in the wall

watching first her sister invade the house—that was bad enough—now the doctor and his patient

she rallies—I can see her—he has given her a purpose—though where does that leave me—us

to this new woman's infirmities she is fresh and alive—but she too is ill and I am her illness—cutting off her options—forcing her to stay when she could have left

now the house is filling with people—if I weren't here she could get on with helping them—instead I distract her—worse—put her in danger

Yes, she calls, I'll be down in a minute. Just looking for a hair pin.

Another letter. Quickly, read while there's no one in the room. Then wishes she hadn't. Why does he taunt her like this.

You were always a wolf in sheep's clothing, master of disguise, but when did you become such a disgusting brute. The indignities of living in close quarters with filthy men has pushed you over the edge. God knows what you spend your days talking about. How can you write these obscenities. No, I most definitely would not like it. Any of what you suggest. Whatever gave you that idea.

Soon, you write. I wish you'd give a date. Not knowing is torture. Never would be too soon.

We have learnt to be well here. Do you really care. Being well is a state of mind. Well in our intimacy, in our love. Close-knit despite life outside falling apart. Well in our common cause for survival.

Reading your letters I see there are terrors worse than war. Who'd have thought it.

The back of things. The back of a year. That will be good. The back of her sister would be welcome but less likely. Everything is conspiring against her. Against him under the stairs. Little human contact now apart from the brush of fingers as she quickly lowers food into the box, pulls out the pot.

Under the step this evening, despair distorts his beautiful features. I miss you. I need you.

I can't, she says. We mustn't give you away. There are too many people around.

The weather doesn't help. Wilder than ever, it has killed all hope that Encarna will come back. The doctor knows nothing about her, or what happened to the people who left town. News can't travel on impassable roads. The wind blows it beyond the hills.

Snow swirling, cracked windows, and no clothes are up to the task of keeping anyone warm. The fireflies, señora Rojas murmurs so feebly no one hears. I don't hear them anymore. She is sitting by the wall under the stairs, where the doctor suggested. As far from the door as possible, under blankets brought from her demolished house. They weigh more than she does. Are the fireflies gone, she mumbles before resuming the next mystery of the Rosary.

mouth—throat—sandpaper in the heat

holding position for hours—days—weeks—like flies dropping one after another—my comrades

we have lost—well lost Brunete and still we are forced to hold fast

hell is knowing that you are utterly dispensable—the stink of that

sometimes the women surprised us—skirts clinging to their thighs—or loose-fitting trousers—the ones who wanted to look like men—working clothes as if they'd just come out in their aprons to feed the hens—cocked rifle aimed

steady—sizzling in hell

their bodies shuddered with the recoil but they held firm—some slim but fearless—others robust—more resolute than some of the men

one beside me—I would like to remember her name now—did I even know it then as we crawled towards the summit—southern eyes fixed on a target and she turned to me—determination in the swift nod—a nod that meant go—I'll cover you

maybe we are equal—they more than us when everything is at stake

Mamá, if we don't have the New Year's Eve grapes does that mean we won't have good luck next year, Alicia wants to know.

Señora Rojas stirs under the blankets. And at the hour of our death. Sloe gin would be lovely.

They look at her in surprise. Usually, she looks more dead than alive. The children giggle, but at some point everyone unravels. Tonight it's Julita. No one sees it coming.

Maybe, if the hundreds of army supply trucks had not got stuck on the road from Valencia because of the frightful weather, there might be grapes, she says.

It's true, the doctor agrees, but—

As if we can take more bad luck. This year alone my Antonio, my boys, my house. Yours too, Doctor. And señora Rojas's. My neighbours, gone. Encarna too. Dead or gone.

Yes, Julita, but let's not—

So many men wounded and dying at the front. Thousands. Thousands. We don't know what our children are going through. And civilians holding out in Madrid against the forces of evil. Much longer than us. Even the animals are gone. Have you seen there are no more dogs in the streets. Where are the dogs. And there has been no one to tend the orchards and farms all summer, now that we need food more than ever. How is it ever going to be put back together again. How. Explain that to me.

The lament gains momentum and even the children are struck by her outburst. Rooted to their chairs. When Julita runs out of things to say no one has answers or consolation.

María turns to Alicia. The grapes don't matter, darling. They are just symbols. One is as good as the next. Look, why don't we pretend we have grapes and on each strike of the clock at midnight, we'll pretend to put a grape in our mouths.

Sceptical looks. Sullen.

Julita, slumped back on the chair, offers no response.

That's an excellent idea, the doctor tries to encourage. But no one is in the mood for pretence.

Good God, María, it's the middle of the night. What are you doing up.

Nothing. I couldn't sleep. What are *you* doing up.

I thought I heard a knock. It startled me.

There's a gale blowing out there. Of course you heard a knock.

How come you're emptying the chamber pot at this hour.

You're going to wake the whole house, Julita.

Is that a new pot. I haven't seen it before.

I keep it under the bed in case I need it. Julita, go back to bed.

Two pots. Well that's a bit extravag… If you have two pots why do you need to empty one in the middle of the night.

I'm going back to bed, Julita. You should do the same.

Rats, señora Rojas shudders under her blankets. Something by the wall under the stairs. On the other side of the wall. She hears it.

Alone in the dark, she lies awake on her mat. The fussy woman and the quiet one think she is comfortable, getting the last of the heat in the room, but they don't know the kitchen walls grow higher at night. Darker, they chatter and creak in dialects she has never heard. Sometimes she hears them cry out.

This is not her house, so why is she here. Is it daytime yet. Blessed art thou amongst women.

Peace, the sooner the better. For the country and the family. It seems simple enough, yet the prospect is remote. It will take years to rebuild the town, clear out the ghosts. Probably many of those who have left will never come back. There's nothing to come back to.

Julita's melancholy has passed, replaced by the litanies that usually keep her going. Talking, talking, talking about nothing and everything, accompanied by her clickety click. It's not a bad way to keep thought out. Everyone gets through it as best they can.

Plain row, clear the table, sweep the floor. Purl row, tape the windows, chop that chair we left in the shed. Plain row, help your mother air the mattresses. Purl row, fetch me the other needles, the thicker ones. Plain row, clear the snow outside the door. We'll be buried alive in here.

Do you like having a sister, Alicia whispers to her mother.

a bowl of rice to last the day—three almonds—will she be able to get another bowl to me tomorrow

fear of hunger—fear of running out of food—already two days ago it happened even though I ration carefully

endurance requires imagination

I think of our rations at the front—but there was always someone to share grievances with—there was light—always someone with cigarettes—someone with a story of how they found food or survived without it—the story of Tena who suckled from the breast of a young woman in one of the villages—in the grain loft—sweetest milk—better than our prized tins of condensed milk—how the woman stroked his head as he suckled while tears streamed down her face

howls of lust and laughter among the men

sometimes you just have to believe in things—in food being plentiful again—in a woman's love—in sanity being restored

fried onions—peppers—green and red—rosemary—thyme—chorizo—tomatoes—chickpeas—carrots and celery—barley—rice—rabbit—fresh baked bread

twice my plate blasted out of my hand—what little there was—gone

on the long marches hoping for bins—a carcass—fruit and vegetable peels—it didn't matter whose mouth they had been in—what dog had chewed those bones

WE BUY

Shirts, belts, garters, ties,
handkerchiefs & similar.
Sepúlveda 66, 11am to 1pm

Thinking about bartering things she won't need. Letting go. Painful because of the weight of memories. Because of the absence it might create. She has waited many months because there is something so final about letting go. It entails a change of direction. The unknown. But there are more pressing things needed, and some memories are best forgotten.

Three cigars

Cigar box with copper etching on the lid

Tie he wore for their wedding

Sunday shoes

Linen handkerchiefs she embroidered for his birthday

Two leather belts

Good to be rid of these. They will be better off as rice, flour, beans, candles. Blankets if there are any to be had.

Blades she found in the children's room and felt a surge of joy. Disproportionate to the items, slightly blunt as they were. That's what life on the edge does. Emotions out of kilter.

You should see the mess in the children's room, she laughed with him under the stairs. Old cables, empty bottles of lotion. All from the barber's shop, they tell me, where they've been playing. It's like Aladdin's cave up there. I know you'd prefer blades for the safety razor, but this will do, won't it.

No break from his work but this morning the doctor requests Tomás and Manolo's help. An industrious man. Observant of people's strengths. His solution to Julita's needs and everyone else's sanity has been a stroke of genius. Señora Rojas is now the main focus of Julita's prattle while she knits. He encourages, confirming that the old woman looks better, her heart rate has improved. Could that be true. Despite the cold, she emerges from under the blankets. Shy turtle from under its shell. Neck circumference and arm lengths need to be measured for cardigans. God is good, she mutters in retreat.

She should have known entertainment is not the doctor's style but she was mistaken to think it was purely an educational outing for the boys. Here they are, back again, red faced pulling a stretcher. The doctor returns her stupefied look with a smile. Don Millán, he introduces the old man on the stretcher, and his daughter, Fina. A woman in a fur coat and hat negotiates the snow some meters behind them. Not in the usual way. Not trudging and slipping and panting. It's hard to say, but there's something different about this woman's steps. Dignity. Or pride.

María has never been conscious of blinking before. Eyelids are a curious phenomenon, working away at regular intervals. Like the beat of a heart. She can't believe this woman, Fina, is wearing court shoes. In the snow. Maybe she has no boots. But still.

Don Millán is in good health were it not for the arthritis that cripples him. They were living in the cellar of their house, the doctor explains, with no light and few provisions.

It doesn't make sense. Why does she become speechless just when she has most to say. Words are clogged again, in her head and in her throat.

Fina reaches her, humble in gratitude, breathing calmly as if the snowdrifts and rubble have taken little out of her.

Gratitude, yes, but what about sleep, María wants to ask. Where will they all sleep. How. Not even these simple questions reach her mouth. And they say silence is consent.

Doctor García left early. The blizzards have stopped and his patients need him. The makeshift hospital at the station is overflowing with men. Frostbite, apart from other injuries. Never seen anything like it, he frowns. After the hospital, he goes house to house. Firewood, he announces this evening, leaving two stools by the door, and they know someone didn't make it through the night.

Fina, he says in his quiet way, will you go to this address tomorrow. I left the door off the latch. There are vegetables, pickles, condensed milk. I think I saw wine too. No one is going to claim it and hopefully no one will have been in looting between now and then. The boys should go with you. There's enough for two baskets at least. This will be timely for the Epiphany.

Fina hesitates. Will they be celebrating it, Doctor. In this house, I mean.

We must stand up for what we believe, Fina.

It's just that... Julita is very against the idea. You know she is strongly Republican. We were talking about it the other day and she reminded me of the fate of Juan Rovira Roure. You know, the lawyer who was executed under government orders for giving the go-ahead to the Epiphany parade.

We are living in very difficult times, Fina.

I must say, Doctor—

Julián. Please call me Julián, he says with a smile.

Julián, Fina smiles at him. Having lived away from Spain for fifteen years, I feel I've lost touch with these extreme sensitivities. It wasn't like this when I left. I don't want to upset anyone, but the views of each sister are so opposed, I have no doubt I'll offend one of them no matter what I do.

Do you know, the doctor looks at her intently, every time I go past the tower of San Martín, with its beautiful mudéjar workmanship, I think how we accommodated Muslims, Jews and Christians here for so many centuries in relative peace. And now it's brother against brother.

And sister against sister, Fina sighs.

We must find a way, at least in this house, to accommodate everyone. There is good will here, Fina, kindness from both sisters.

so alone in the midst of so many people

food at least—between one of his patients or another he seems to have access to food—not much but better than before—blankets too and old furniture

Manolo chops the furniture for firewood—a good lad—I'm proud of him—I would give anything to put my arms around him and give him a big hug—he's so thoughtful with Tomás and Alicia— they adore him even though he's so quiet—judicious—it gives him a kind of gravitas

is anything spared the destruction of war—some beautiful pieces—finely turned wood and marquetry—but this new woman—Fina—nods approval as Manolo looks at her one last time before bringing down the axe

Pretending to be busy with the hens in the shed every morning so she can intercept the postman. Hide the letters before going into the house, the way the hens hide their eggs.

You're going to turn into a chicken one of these days, Julita admonishes. What on earth takes you so long out there.

María leaves the basket of eggs on the counter. Four this morning, and goes upstairs.

Instead of a letter, this picture. Three kings on camels approaching a manger because of the festive season. Hills in the background. A single star in the sky. Hand drawn outlines lightly pencilled, over and over.

For emphasis. Is that what it is. To show concentration, attention to detail. Or does it show dissatisfaction with the first and second and third lines sketched. Tracing over the lines to improve them. You never showed any talent for drawing before. Am I to believe you did this yourself. That you did it for me. Is it meant to make up for the abominable sentiments of your last letter. Give with one hand. Take with the other.

I am loath to call you a liar even in my mind. Set you off.

The hills of the Jarama valley, you say these are, because that is where you saw true Arabs for the first time. Franco's Army of Africa, riding to redeem Spain the way king Balthazar rode from Asia to honour the redeemer. It's strange to see on paper how you twist words the way you twist everything else.

But you were good at the twisted, honeyed words. And I was a fool.

these letters here for safekeeping since Julita moved into her room—though why she doesn't throw them out I don't know

Alicia squeezed between the sisters with the boys on the floor at the foot of the bed—I picture it as she describes it—five bodies like we used to sleep in my mother's village—all the cousins on the floor—endless days of childhood

no chance of going upstairs now—the soft bed would be so welcome—but I mustn't think of myself—she is the one risking everything

these letters—she has explained their arrogance—to think I never knew—no one did

who are we when we are alone with our thoughts

I miss her more than ever even though she's on the other side of the wall—miss her touch

I need her

I will never get out of here now but I would if he ever—I would kick down the wall and strangle him with my bare hands

Slowly spooning the broth with all eyes on him round the table. Tonight's news raises their spirits.

The poor donkey was killed by flying debris, the doctor tells them. Up by the north wall. If you're quick in the morning you might be lucky. Tell my colleague that I sent you.

Donkey, Alicia exclaims in horror.

Horse, donkey, cat, dog... Meat is meat, the doctor smiles at her. Protein. It tastes much the same. A bit of meat wouldn't be bad, now, would it, he winks at Alicia. One of you ladies should go. Bring the boys, but avoid the town centre at all costs. The bullets are constant around the square.

A working donkey, was it, don Millán wants to know. That's a significant loss.

There are worse things to lose, the doctor says. Besides, we should make the most of the little mercies that come our way. Better than let the animal fill someone else's stomach, don't you think.

Rats, she insists, tucking her arm back under the blanket. By the wall. I was sitting—

You're not to worry, señora Rojas. You are safe here. If there are any rats, Manolo will catch them. I've heard in some places they've resorted to eating them. Disgusting, but needs must. Well, we won't be doing that. Not when we can have donkey instead.

Señora Rojas gives her a puzzled look. I'll get Manolo to make a trap anyway, Julita reassures her. He might be able to make it from pieces of old furniture, or tins, or something. He's good that way. Would you like me to heat up that stone now that the fire is blazing. I think you're getting cold. We can't have you getting cold.

No, I think—

No problem. I'll heat it up for you later. As long as you're warm enough, that's the main thing. Anyway, this shawl I'm knitting for you will be nice and warm.

It doesn't matter what windows are shattered, how cold the kitchen gets, the shortage of food, the encampment the house has become. Routines are built regardless. Like empires. Order keeps the day moving forward with purpose so they can still feel human.

Making beds. Cleaning the kitchen. Feeding the hens. Collecting eggs. Stoking the fire. Chopping wood. Knitting. Braiding hair. Selecting ribbons. Writing letters to Fernando and José. Cooking. Eating. Wiping down the table. Darning socks. Reading the paper. Discussing the progress of the Popular Front. Lamenting the war. Telling the children fairy tales. Sweeping the floor. Sewing a button. Playing cards.

Doing nothing takes all day and plenty of energy.

Well, well… Such a spotless, orderly house. This is better than a hotel, the doctor pronounces when he comes back. Most of them have never been in a hotel but they imagine vases of flowers, velvet drapes, chandeliers, and it is as if the room has been transformed and they are living in luxury.

Epiphanies. There are few these days.

Three men on camels crossing the desert to pay homage to a new born who turned out to be a rebel. Was his mother proud of her son's defiance. Turning his back on traditional life, on a wife, on their ancient religion. Born into bleak circumstances, like little Inés. Forced to flee, like so many here. If it had to be a choice, what would a mother prefer. For her child to die an infant or become a renegade, condemned as a criminal. What would you choose, María. What would you choose.

And there it is. The epiphany. Lying in the crowded bed, surrounded by the acrid pheromones of these growing boys, she suddenly considers herself fortunate. Fortunate she never had to choose.

Those men on their camels in a time of peace. What did they believe. Magical things, no doubt. Shooting stars and the mythologies of the skies. Like her mother taught her when she was a child. Belief in something. Ritual. The comfort of structures. Cling to it for dear life.

Avoiding the floorboards that creak, she zigzags across the room. Downstairs. There may just be time to empty his pot. His face appears from the darkness under the step. A kiss, she whispers, is all I have for you, my love. I want you to know I love you so much I could burst.

Then I have the universe and everything in it, he says. What more could—

Creaking upstairs. Hurriedly she kisses him. I'll come to you tonight, and she replaces the slat. The creaking won't be Julita. She has vowed to stay away from any celebration of the Epiphany. María suppresses a giggle. If ever there was proof that God exists, this is it. A day without Julita dominating.

Shaving bowl and brush for Manolo.

Linen handkerchief for Tomás.

Coloured ribbons for Alicia to tie up her hair.

They are giddy when Fina appears. Queenly, she descends in her long velvet housecoat. Where did she get such a beautiful robe.

I would like to offer you another gift, she tells them. It's not a thing. It's a little piece of myself.

The gift of the unexpected. A book. I've had it since I lived in Paris, she reminisces, *Five Thousand French Idioms*. I would like to teach you French and about France and the artists and dancers who live there. The ones I knew, at any rate. Only if you would like to hear. And I can teach you maths and geography. What do you think.

Alicia takes the book out of Fina's hand. Opens it on the page with her age, nine, and selects the idiom with her mother's age, thirty-three. *Tout va bien!*

Paris. The word is lingering in the kitchen. But of course, they had forgotten Fina lived in Paris. It explains why everything about her is different.

I was a dancer, she says, and they stare in surprise, unable to imagine such a thing. I left Spain during Primo de Rivera's dictatorship. There were no prospects here for a dancer anyway. But I came back some years ago when Mamá died. Papá needs me. My sisters have their own families in Barcelona and can't be here. I taught French at the Liceo until it closed because of the war.

I want to be a dancer, Alicia declares with sudden passion.

You will make a great dancer, Fina smiles.

Doctor García joins the mesmerised group. Does anyone escape Fina's spell, he wonders, forcing his gaze away from her. I have something for the children too, he announces, pulling an old stethoscope he no longer uses out of his doctor's bag. The excitement fizzes.

I want to be a doctor, Tomás declares.

Me too, his sister shouts. I want to be a doctor.

You just said you wanted to be a dancer, Tomás says, to everyone's amusement and for a moment no one is thinking of the war.

One by one they are subjected to his medical examinations. The heartbeat of someone laughing is faster than the heartbeat of their aunt knitting in the bed upstairs. Legs have no heartbeats, Tomás announces amid their laughter, and neither do bums.

Don Millán wants to know if they can hear anything inside his head, but they can't. As I thought, he taps his head, brain dead. And the children double over.

entertaining as it is I can't enter the spirit of the day—Uribe gnaws at my mind—some celebrate while others die and it grates

others who were once very much alive

you must come visit—he would say—when the war is over

the sea in Valencia—he said—it stretches forever—in summer it sparkles like diamonds—out on my father's fishing boat—I'll take you out

he encouraged with his humour—especially before an attack— *qui no vullga pols que no vaja a l'era*—if you don't want to get dusty don't go into the field—and out we'd go to face the enemy with a smile on our faces

as if we had a choice

it's a deal—he said—you're coming to visit me in Valencia

the more unlikely we knew this to be the more we nodded—the more we nodded the more exaggerated his hospitality became— the bigger the paella his wife was going to make

Home has shed its familiarity, its privacy. In some strange way it no longer belongs to her anymore even though the newcomers treat her with respect and the doctor, especially, thanks her for sheltering his patients. It has become a place that vaguely resembles her home, where she is a lodger with strangers at the table, food appearing out of nowhere, conversations that would never before have been heard in this kitchen, Julita often ignoring her for a change. Before all this, the house had been part of her, but now it is as if she has been excised from it, adrift among these people. An observer of the strange world that has emerged since the town came under siege, dizzied by its extremes.

If only they would leave. If silence could be restored. If there was a pill that might suppress the need to cry. Or scream.

Through the merriment, she knows he will be enjoying their happiness, wishing like her that they would all just go away.

Did you kill anyone, she wants to ask him under the stairs.

A simple question but the words refuse to collaborate. There is accusation in them even if it's not intended. Disrespect towards the inherent goodness in him.

Did you...

Were you ever...

At any point, if your superiors issued a command...

What would happen if...

Curious how words can have a separate existence of their own. To spare us, could that be it.

She will never know because she will never ask. Sometimes it's better not to know.

everything swirling in my head—thoughts and more thoughts

what if I had stayed longer in school—learnt more about each of the factions—what Fina tells them about president Azaña— privilege blinds him to the lives of most of us—to my simple life before this—the smallest rights that should be ours

I wish I'd had a teacher like her—to have learnt more about the countries surrounding Spain—their mountains—rivers

would I have done things differently—would I have understood people better—them—us—myself

would I have realised the Republic is doomed with the fanciful leaders it cobbles together—and the misguided and the selfish and the pursuers of power—aghghgh

endless questions—to my detriment because from here it looks like my entire life has been a mistake—the entire course of Spain is a mistake

would I have settled for the first pretty girl

in the dark I have no choice but to think and rethink all of this

she told them about Cervantes the other day—how he honed his thoughts in prison—ha—that I understand—I know how that feels

we are all a little bit mad

It's hard not to be anxious. Has he been wounded, arrested, worse. Will he be back at all. Maybe something happened at the hospital. Maybe a baby is struggling to enter the madness. Round and round, unpleasant thoughts, furrowed brows.

The stethoscope is in the children's corner with their books and Fina laughs. I wonder how fast our hearts are beating now. Julita smirks without taking her eyes off the knitting needles.

They busy themselves with nothing. Creep upstairs to check on the children. Clickety click. María smooths her skirt. Chairs are rearranged. They pace. Check what's left in the larder. Set a place at the table for whenever the doctor comes back. Stick down curled edges on the tape that barely holds the windows intact. Move the fork further to the right for symmetry.

What would we be doing now if the war had never happened. What if.

The stillness of a hypothetical other life settles over them. I would have my Antonio and my own house, says Julita, instead of being stuck here.

Would you have been happier, María ventures.

Clickety click a fraction faster. We had a good marriage, Julita retorts. I loved my Antonio, may he rest in peace. Now look what you made me do. I've lost count.

She wouldn't know what love was if it was staring her in the face.

But it would be cruel to say this. As long as she can be the boss of everyone and everything, she's happy. Maybe bossing is what Julita calls love. Taking over the house might be an act of love.

what does anyone know

I loved my Antonio she says—did she really—it looked so different from how María and I love each other

is it the heart—the head—the liver—this box

how is it that this—this impossible thing my life has become— this is love—very little before it comes close

in the gut—the purity of it—the intensity—the resilient quiet of it

the way she opens the house—allows them all to be—makes room for foibles—tempers—laughter

love

I never saw it as starkly before—never saw Julita as she really is— never saw María—though I was attracted to her steadfastness— she has taught me so much about love in this unbearable tomb—about its essence stripped of everything—her dignity in all of this—the compassion and caring while she negotiates everyone's needs—mine—her own

to think I was married and knew nothing of women—had I not ended up here I would have forever been a slave to my old assumptions about men and women—slave to my slovenly efforts at manliness

I see more clearly in the dark—looking back sometimes hurts

He was needed at the hospital because they ran out of supplies, now grateful for the food they have prepared. The medical truck should have arrived three days ago but ran into drifts in Torres de Utiel. Hope was dwindling, patients getting weaker. Some died. But tonight, at the eleventh hour, a woman arrived. Dr Mercedes Maestres. Her name is in every sentence he speaks. Dr Mercedes Maestres had been travelling with the truck. Her bravery still lights his face and the women wonder what it would be like to have followed other paths, lived braver lives.

A selfless decision to walk from Torres de Utiel with the supplies, he tells them, oblivious to the dangers, freezing temperatures, hunger, tiredness. The doctor shakes his head in admiration. Sheltered wherever she could on the way, walking for miles, thinking only of how urgent the supplies were. By the time she reached us she needed medical attention herself, for frostbite, dehydration, but she would have none of it. Insisted on helping with the patients.

We had to tend to everyone tonight, he says, but we managed to administer medication, change dressings, do transfusions. Thank goodness the nuns were with us. They never sleep, those women. They just keep giving and giving with a smile on their faces, holding the men's hands in their final moments, or when we're out of anaesthetic. It took a while tonight, but there's a great sense of accomplishment. So many of the men will now recover. Tonight, we defied the war. And the weather.

He is living here, María thinks, talking to us every day, and we know nothing about him, really.

No sooner has Fina sat down with her father this morning to shave him than the old man starts sobbing. It comes without warning. Quietly at first, he bites his bottom lip to stanch the flow. Then is powerless and they come, bitter, bitter tears. Like geese, the women flock. The children too. A severe pain, perhaps. But physical pain produces a different type of sound. They know it even as they enquire. This is a different convulsion. The darkness they are all enduring but dare not express. If they did, they might fall forever into its abyss. That black hole where nostalgia and grief and regret make themselves at home. Besides, there is no instant cure for pains of that kind. Stealthily they invade, settle over time in pores and cells, deeper and deeper. It's useless to ignore them. They persist and surface in unexpected ways.

The women and the children watch, unable to stop don Millán's transformation. He is no longer himself. He has become someone he didn't know he was, his grief whittled from all the precious moments of life that can never be lived again. Fina puts her arm around him. *Papá, qué te duele.* Are you in pain. There is no embarrassment as they watch his tears because they are also theirs, and of the man in the street and the woman in the next village. Communal tears flowing all over this country. This carnage that no one can fix, no matter who wins. Tighter she holds him as he shakes. It's alright, Papá, don't cry.

Every day it gets harder to bear the cold. She has to heat stones and wrap them in muslin to warm up don Millán's bed mat in the landing. Señora Rojas's too.

When are we going home, the old lady asks.

We're very well here, don Millán reassures her. We must be thankful, to the doctor and this family.

I pray all the time, señora Rojas says, fingering her beads. For everyone. That it ends soon.

Don Millán sighs. It will end, he nods. Sooner or later.

Did you hear that, she asks, looking suddenly alert. Rats.

There are no rats here, señora. It's the children. Look.

Jumping jacks and stretching under Fina's tutelage. A daily routine. Leapfrogging. Running on the spot.

All this flapping about, Julita scolds, and skipping in the middle of the kitchen... It's very irritating, Fina. The children would be better off doing something useful. Look at them, they're all flushed and breaking out in a sweat. The kitchen is not the place for these antics.

It's important in the absence of other exercise, Fina explains, now that they can't be outside running around.

Julita shakes her head. Please, they're too old for running around.

Not too old for exercise to get the blood flowing. It builds their strength.

María smiles towards the wall. There is something encouraging about Fina's naivety in believing she might persuade Julita. As if logic or some other way of doing things could possibly prevail.

She hasn't felt this mischievous since she was a child. Fina, would you mind if I joined in the exercises from now on, María asks. It seems like a good way to get warm.

She doesn't need to see Julita behind her to know the way her facial muscles are twitching. Don Millán, too, finds himself smiling.

the pain is constant now—shoulders—back—legs

no relief—not standing or sitting—or kneeling and stretching forward

not kneeling with arms stretched over my head

not rolling my shoulders

not the step forward step back to the right to the left

the trench was a luxury compared to this—what was I thinking

sometimes I have no interest in what goes on in the room—it worries me

I can hear it all even when I'd rather peace and quiet—the incessant chatter—how can they be so loud—the children riotous in the mornings

I need to get out—need to walk—need to breathe—I cn't brth

Cabaret is Fina's word. A Parisian world that sends ripples around the kitchen.

Feathers, Julita exclaims when Fina announces her plan. It sounds…distasteful. Inappropriate. Kicking legs in the air. We have our perfectly lovely folk jigs from Aragón. Why can't the children do a traditional *jota* instead of some…some foreign thing.

It's much more than dancing. It's a variety of performances. I will be sensitive to the children's own abilities and sensiti—

It doesn't sound suitable for children at all. There's no practical application for that kind of activity. The traditional songs and dances are different, they're part of our culture, but why something so…so outlandish. If Alicia was my daughter, I wouldn't have her embarrass herself with this vulgarity.

Stricken, Alicia turns to her mother. Please, Mamá, can we.

Can you what.

Put on a show.

What.

A show, Mamá. Alicia pleads while Julita looks at her sister. Mute. Is it disapproval or a quizzical grimace.

Oh, a show, María blinks. Yes, of course, why not. I'm sorry, I wasn't following the conversation. I have a headache.

There's more than a headache wrong with your head. How can you let the child take part in this, this…

La P-a-r-i-s-i-e-n-n-e. Don Millán makes the word linger, as if speaking to a beautiful memory. We would never learn anything if we only limit ourselves to what we already know. A dancer is stronger than you'll ever be, he says to Julita, and strength, as you know, is a very useful thing in these times. There is no reprimand in his tone. He is simply stating what is obvious to him. Stamina too, he tells her, dancers know all about that. Fina has been independent all her life. She knows—

Papá, there's no need. Please.

There is. This lady doesn't understand that you—

This lady is Julita, Papá, she's our friend. She has been very kind to us.

Yes, you are right, but she doesn't know how hard the work of a dancer is, bringing joy to people. She thinks it's outlandish. A waste of time. His voice is kind, almost a lullaby. You mustn't judge my daughter, dear lady.

Out of respect for don Millán's seniority, Julita contains herself. Lets the tension pull just below the surface and María has not felt as calm since they all arrived. It gives her strength, of a different kind than the strength of dancers. Although, maybe it comes from a similar place.

Well, I am very curious about this cabaret, María says. The performers will perform, and if anyone doesn't want to watch the show, they don't have to. They can go upstairs. Now, excuse me, I have a splitting headache.

This letter she cannot stuff quickly enough back in the envelope. Into the drawer until she can take them downstairs. Quickly she calculates. Six or seven weeks.

February, you say. End of the month.

You can't come here. I must stop shaking. Someone will wonder what's wrong with me. You can't come here. I don't want you to.

Knots in my stomach. I can barely speak. How would it be with all these people. It wouldn't work.

There are so many ways to kill. Me, you killed in broad daylight and I didn't even realise it.

We must think of a plan. Get him out and leave. With the children. Where. Everywhere is a battlefield. Abroad. France. Yes, France. That's what we'll do. But how do we get him out. We can't. We must.

Despair the moment the step slides back and he sees her face. There is no time for her to comment or for him to offer reassurance. Words he wants to say. Words he keeps thinking of saying, stories to share, concerns to discuss, but they never have time together anymore. He is less than a thing under the stairs. An irritant, perhaps, though her plaintive look tells him maybe not. He takes the letter and the slat is pressed back in place.

people—everyone I knew—people I greeted in the village every day

where are they now—I would ask them things—anything—have a conversation about nothing—the weather

things that used to bother me—the leaky outhouse—Tonto chewing on my chair

harsh words over small things

unspoken words

incomplete actions and thoughts—I should have—why do we not

at least I told María I loved her—I told her I had loved her from the moment I saw her—from the first time I went to her parents' house

the mattress makes her real—I feel it as if she were here snuggled up beside me—this dent where she lay—the angle of the cushion—I move my fingers over the mattress—the cushion— stroking as if they are her—remembering everything—everything

strange how absence can be filled

Curlers in her hair last night. This morning painted nails and she went to the Communist building even though it's Saturday. María raised an eyebrow but thought no more of it.

Yet, this evening, there is a dreamy look on Julita's face, a serenity that María has seen before and ignored. Why did she ignore it. Now she can't. This evening it speaks to her, like clouds dispersing and the sky becoming clear again.

Packing provisions, Julita replies. Usually she doesn't even have to be asked. Usually she natters on about how hard they've worked and the invaluable service they are providing. Not this evening. Pensive silence and the truth of it starts to fall into place.

The stranger. The man Julita danced with in the town square. María recalls him vividly now. How he held her. Handsome. How familiar Julita was with him. He helped carry a bag of coal back to the house. Watching her sister drift upstairs, the extra provisions she brings back from the Communist building begin to take on a worrying significance. It started around that time and she never thought to question it. But this evening all the pieces are sliding into place with Julita's wistful look. Alarmingly so. Julita and a Republican soldier. She wouldn't bring him back to the house, surely. María's heart skips a beat. Maybe she's reading too much into it.

From cold house to hothouse. Undercurrents of resentment over nothing. How long should stones be heated. Which songs are patriotic, which are not. Loud snoring. What the order of privilege is regarding bathwater.

Morale is a fragile thing. Like happiness.

He's quite sure, the doctor tells her. He is one of the militiamen who used to frequent Joselito's bar before Encarna left. That's how I recognised him in the hospital. He says Encarna was among a group of people captured on their way out of town the day of the amnesty. He saw it with his own eyes but could do nothing. It's a blessing you didn't go with her.

Captured by whom. María is appalled, confused, indignant. I thought they had the fascist rebels under control in the hills, or wherever they are.

It wasn't the fascists. The doctor looks at her squarely, hoping he won't have to explain.

Things he has been telling her under the stairs come crashing into her head. Talk of armed militias killing people for no reason. *Vamos a dar un paseito.* Let's take a little walk. Everyone knows by now that there's no coming back from that invitation. Once, he said, they put a man in prison for chopping down a tree for firewood. Could it be true.

Encarna never did anything except welcome those men, María says.

Everyone with money was taken, the doctor is speaking as gently as he can. Having money makes you an enemy of the people, it seems, and from the militiaman's account she had quite a substantial amount. I will do what I can to find out where she is.

What will happen to her. Where did they take her.

He doesn't know. As I say, I will try to find out and see if we can persuade the authorities to release her.

Authorities, she scoffs. What authorities. Is the government now authorising the capture of old ladies who have lost everything in this godforsaken country except for the miserable pittance they've managed to save after a lifetime of hard work. Defenceless old ladies. You couldn't make it up. You can be sure those men were acting on no authority. They're not even proper soldiers. Just bumpkins posturing and swaggering. Didn't I see them in the bar every day. They're all that anarchist bunch taking the law into their own hands. They should be ashamed of themselves. How did this happen, Doctor. How did we get to this.

Why does everything seem much worse at night. In bed she trembles, racking her brain for what seems like hours. She shouldn't have poured out her misgivings like that. The doctor said nothing. Calm throughout, he listened, and it bothers her now. Reassurance that he'd search for Encarna. But has he ever given an opinion on the war. Every conversation they have had, his chats with don Millán after dinner in the evening, everything is flooding her mind tonight. There is nothing there. No sense of his loyalty. Details of his patients, yes. Conditions at the hospital. Encouragement with the way she and Julita take care of señora Rojas and don Millán. Gratitude. All these things, and he laments the war, for sure, but in a general sort of way. Why did she never notice before.

Are you still awake, Julita whispers across Alicia.

Sorry, I can't sleep, María whispers back.

Stop tossing and turning. You're keeping me awake.

She curls on her side and stares at the wall. He has never expressed allegiance for one side or the other, has he.

The only one who has ever been to a cabaret is Fina, but Saturday is here. It has taken years to arrive because now that they are housebound, each day is longer than a year. They've all turned out for the spectacle, having witnessed the years of rehearsing, intrepid outings to Fina and don Millán's old house to rescue a gramophone and heavy slate records from the cellar, feathered fans, a small lamp with tassels, candlesticks, a top hat, more high heels, old newspapers.

Years to transform the kitchen into a cabaret and still no one knows what a cabaret is. A place with dim lighting and colourful costumes. Julita wants to say it has undertones of brothel, but she wouldn't like the children to hear such a word. A place where music is more important than work. A place where Fina has become half swan, half palm tree, and newspapers become paper flowers, lanterns, birds. Tomás has pulled one, a dove, out of the top hat. Fanfare suits him. How did he do that, señora Rojas wants to know, but no one hears her above the din of Alicia's fandango. Clop and stomp of shoes that are too big for her but there is duende in the ruffle of her skirt, arms aloft. The adults are transfixed. Accompanied by the gramophone, Manolo sings the lyrics in a sweet tenor voice no one knew he had. The swan tree now introduces a poem, Life's a Dream, by the renaissance master Calderón, one of their favourites. The children recite a stanza each to enthusiastic applause and reminiscences of school days.

Even Julita begins to warm to this hodgepodge Paris thing. Sealed with a traditional Aragonese *jota*, as Julita had requested, a cabaret can almost pass as respectable entertainment. Everyone has entered the spirit of it, singing as the children neatly perform the steps, clacking castanets.

Bis. Bis. Encore.

The snow has stopped falling but not her hopes. Under the stairs, the possibility of stealing away with the children has opened up a new world.

Out of here, his eyes grow bright in the candlelight and he grips her arm. France, yes. We will think about how that could be arranged. My God, I've thought about getting out of here so often, I can't tell you, but only now that you mention it does it seem possible. We will go together. I so desperately need you, María.

He hugs her in the candlelight. The way a drowning man might.

We'll think of something, she says.

It was inevitable. Feet at the top of the stairs stop as she lifts the slat to get out. Ever so cautiously. Silent, feet poised on the edge. Whose. One foot hovering as if about to begin descent.

She freezes, willing herself unseen. Lowers the slat. Their luck was bound to run out. They both knew it but never really expected it for real. Usually people are quiet at night, not wanting to wake the household, but the footsteps that then descend are deliberately heavy, unlike the hovering at the top of the stairs. A warning not to reappear.

The stench of fear fills the box. It claws so thickly she is afraid it will seep through the peephole and the cracks and give them away. If they have not already been discovered. They hold their breath in the box, the maddening pump of blood rushing in their ears. Faster and faster. She holds still for so long she has the impression of having turned to stone.

Directly above them, heavy steps again. Whoever is there will surely lift the slat. Surely out of curiosity. Heart louder. Faster. They are drenched in perspiration. But there is no pause in the upward steps. If she was seen, she is being purposely ignored. How long do they hold still after the footsteps have retreated into one of the bedrooms. Did they even breathe.

A problem with the outhouse requires attention. Wrapped in many layers she comes to see what problem the doctor has found, only to find him standing idly, blowing into his woollen gloves.

She has steeled herself to refuse any more patients. They can't fit anyone else in the house.

For a moment, the doctor stares at his feet. When he looks up at her, his brow is more furrowed than usual. There is no problem. Not with the outhouse. His gaze falls to the ground again, and when she follows it, it hits her. The feet were his and he saw. Why else here at the outhouse, away from everyone's attention.

María, if you need anything, anything at all, I will help you. You are taking care of my patients in your home and I am very grateful.

She thought it would be a relief to have someone share her burden. She had prayed for such a moment, but now she is not so sure. They've spoken about it under the stairs. The doctor, they both agree, would be the best person to confide in if they need outside help. Still, she doesn't know what to say now that he puts it to her. There is no colour left in the world, she thinks, staring at his pale face. Everything has faded to grey. All the colour is buried. Under snow. Under stairs. In a white box.

Thank you, Doctor.

Don't be too proud, María. Anything you say to me will be in confidence. I give you my word.

can they hear my stomach rumbling

a potato is as vital to winning the war as a bullet—who said that—I don't even remember the taste of potatoes—just that I liked them

how much else is it possible to forget

even things I never liked—celery—beetroot—I will never turn down celery again—would it still taste the same—give me a plateful of beetroot now and I would eat it with humility and gratitude

how much longer before she can get something to me—I'm starving—and to think that with the food Julita brings they have more than before—the smell is killing me through the cracks

Santa Ursula and her eleven thousand virgins. No one knows who they were. Imagine beheading eleven thousand women because they believe something you don't. One. Two. Seventeen. And another. Six thousand eight hundred and fifty-four. Six thousand eight hundred and fifty-five. On and on. How long would that take. Ten thousand nine hundred and ninety-nine. Weeks. One more. Eleven thousand. Done.

Surely not. But regardless of how many, did they have a choice, the beheaders and the beheaded.

The comrades offer no choice about who enters Santa Ursula. Even women who stay at home to carry on with the business of living need to be weeded out. Virgins, especially, need weeding out. Virginity is not a choice here. Through the wooden door they arrive, into the cloister that is now called *cheka*. Cloisters are beautiful places, created for light and shade at just the right time of day. Architecture at the service of the soul. Places of contemplation if you can drown out the screams.

Their crimes, the usual: an uncle a priest, a neighbour heard expressing rebel sympathies, a cousin too big for her boots, a suitor rejected, a grandmother heard saying the burning of art was criminal, a brother suspected of hiding potatoes for his own use.

The smell of burnt flesh, familiar in an unfamiliar way as they are pushed down the stairs. Animal, could that be it. From the past when meat was plentiful. Faintly pig. Boar, perhaps. How animal can a human be. Animal down to the soles of their feet, and soles sizzle fast.

Down the steps into the crypt and the stench is overpowering. Excrement and urine and fear. There are men here too, the women learn from the pitch of the roars they hear. The smell of burning flesh and the roars now make sense.

What is it about virgins in particular. About this truckload of bitches, sluts, whores, compared to the women at home.

For those lacking commitment to the Republic there are boxes. Some women are bigger than others. Some men smaller than some women. But they can all curl foetal to fit in a box. A day. A month. Encarna in her box thinks of a womb. Miscarriage. Of children. Of justice. How much a body endures.

Bats. Cudgels. Straps. Fire. Bright lights. Weights. Iron bars. Blades. Bricks. Matchsticks. Water. Vice.

Children, listen to this. Learn, Julita instructs as she reads the newspaper. Look what the Republic is doing for you. They've asked the French government to send a third convoy of food to the Republican troops and milk for the children of Spain.

Will it be chocolate milk.

She was always a spoilt child, she tells señora Rojas under her breath.

Uncomprehending, señora Rojas smiles. Something has triggered a memory. Where's our goat, she asks.

We don't have a goat, señora Rojas. We only have hens.

Papá bought it just the other day. She looks so deflated that even Julita doesn't have the heart to clarify further. Instead, she returns to the newspaper.

Ah, this is what you should have done, María. You should have sent the children to France. It says here that the Spanish children who were evacuated to France are well looked after by their new families, and their parents who have remained in loyal territory can request for them to stay on. Did you never think of doing that. You could have contributed to the war if you didn't have them hanging out of you all the time. Encarna thought you were mad to stay here too.

María, holding the shaving bowl for Fina, doesn't even look up. There's no point. Blades twist in so many ways.

Even though María is listening intently, the doctor's words are disconnected. He says, Encarna. He says, Many women. Road to Sagunto. Money, too much. Not enough. Militias. Snow and Santa Ursula.

The words, she understands. But together, the way they are coming out of his mouth, they make no sense. Santa Ursula. Why would they take her to a convent. Encarna and another woman, she asks.

Encarna and several other women, he repeats.

Is she in the convent now.

Doctor García looks at her. How could she be expected to know about Santa Ursula. As I said, the man I spoke to thought she was taken to Valencia. He saw them on the road out of Sagunto.

His hesitation has alerted her. It's not a convent, is it, she says. Have they turned the convent into a prison. I know they've done that in many places. Is that it, Doctor. She's in prison.

Not officially, no, he replies, and she can tell this means yes. I'm just repeating what I heard. But all may not be lost, María. We mustn't give up hope at this point.

You'd think a prison is a prison is a prison. But no. There are prisons you come out of and prisons you don't. State prisons and Communist prisons and militia prisons and makeshift prisons and understairs prisons and the prisons in your head.

When, she asks, as if it makes any difference.

Not long after she left. Snow. Soon. Chocolate. Must perhaps have been. Changed hands. Money. But you never can tell. Military commander who knows his brother.

Your brother, she asks, trying to sound as if she is following him. Did he actually say *chocolate*.

No. A brother of the man I spoke to. There's no point worrying about it, María. He will do whatever he can. I will try too.

There are more words that make no sense. Or do, in the way a badly known language makes sense, or the words in a dream make sense.

Thank you, Doctor, she says. The smile he gives her seems to confirm that she has understood something.

poor Encarna—few come out of the chekas—I can't tell María—
she didn't properly understand what the doctor was telling her—
how could she

hope at all cost—how we cling to it

even hope in the government despite everything going wrong—
everything a mistake—mistake on top of mistake

mistake to dissolve the army—you have much to answer for José
Giral—much to answer for

mistake to alienate the military so completely

mistake to leave weapons in the hands of the workers'
organisations

mistake to think untrained people would use weapons wisely—
would have the skills and strategy for combat

mistake to think unbridled revenge wouldn't come into it

mistake to think chekas—to think they were shut down months
ago—of course they weren't

LA VANGUARDIA

LA VANGUARDIA Wednesday 12 January 1938   Page 7

VALENCIAN WOMEN AGAINST FASCISM - CONFERENCE

Conclusion Reached

Valencia, 11th – The Provincial Conference of the Women Against Fascism has concluded its deliberations and reached the following conclusions:

One – Request that the Government officially recognise women's right to work full time and contribute to the war effort, to be elaborated on and made effective by the Ministry of National Defence.

Two – Request that the two Main Syndicates deploy their technical expertise in the training of women for various professions, and in so doing ensure that the true centres of education are factories, workshops and fields

Three – Establish houses for the care of infants and kindergartens for older children so that women can have the comfort of knowing their children are cared for during the working day.

Four – Seek a resolution to all problems regarding supplies.

Five – Create medical centres in the countryside and infant hygiene programmes.

Six – Protection for pregnant women and lactating mothers.

Seven – Propose discussing the problem of unity with all women's groups of the vanguard.

Eight – Women Against Fascism promise to combine their aspirations and strengths into the sole aim of winning the war, supporting the Government's decisions in a disciplined way.

Nine – Request that the Government solve the labour and financial problems of the war wounded, as well as of the widows and dependent children of the combatants so that neither become a burden to the State and can engage in active work.

Protection for lactating mothers, he reads. Will any of these requests be met.

She says nothing, not wanting to spoil their brief time together, but the child has taken over. Cries she can hear in this box, as she can so often in the kitchen and in the street. Cries of a fading face. Harder she needs to focus, recall a particular moment, to bring back the face. Of all the deprivations and frustrations this seems the most cruel. Fragments of child. Like all the other fragments. Work, Encarna, the town, her house, these people's lives.

Fragments of legs. She never did fill out. Mouth twisting in her determined search for the barren breast. Cries of protest. Pain compounded by memory slipping away. Only those cardigans in the drawer are proof that she was here.

Beside him on the cushions she is close, but he senses her distance as he peers at the newspaper in candlelight. Arm around her shoulders, under his breath he reads to her: Request that the government officially recognise women's right to work full time and contribute to the war effort. He chuckles. Does knitting count as a contribution to the war effort.

Suddenly distressed, she stirs. I'm sorry, I can't, she shakes her head. Not tonight. With terrifying lack of caution she lifts the slat.

He reaches out, startled. What did I say. Tell me. Please.

Her hand clutches his. Is it love, apology, despair. Then swiftly she is gone and he can't tell which of them is hurting more from the emptiness in her wake.

There is menace in the mist and the town is unrecognisable. Threat lurks everywhere, in doorways, behind pillars, under every pile of rubble, in a furtive glance. Innocent people, surely. Like her. Out trying to find provisions, news. But the pulse of the town is gone, replaced by anxiety that ticks away in artillery fire, punctuated by clouds of dust from crumbling houses. Sky and street meld together.

Shutters down. Chairs that once buzzed with clients outside Joselito's bar lie upended. Glass in the snow. A recent hit. How different everything looks in winter. Or is she confusing winter with war. Bleak, in any case. Hernández & Sons. Finest Quality Shoes. Door hanging on a broken hinge. Windows blown out. First floor beams dangling over ground floor. She so much wanted to get him a pair of slippers. The ones with lambswool inside.

Shelling leaves a hole where something used to be. But not just something physical like houses and shops. Not just craters in the middle of the pavement where trees used to be. It leaves a hole where the heart is too. It is distressing not to recognise the street anymore. As if little bits of her that were here yesterday had disappeared into a hole with the rest of the town. She looks at what last week was Hernández & Sons.

Time races by. Stands still. Was Hernández & Sons here last Wednesday.

The papers are full of words. *Our glorious Army.*

The offensive has been *completely successful. Enemy attacks have been fought off.*

Facts and more facts. Depending on who you talk to.

He says it's not true. He says the papers are full of lies. She believes him. He's been there.

It's not just people dying, she thinks. It's trust and truth. And no one seems to care.

But no. That's not true either.

Anything you can remember, the doctor urges. However trivial. It may be of use. Did she have family.

María can't think of what might be useful information. Encarna had no children of her own. I never asked, Doctor. Some things are private.

What about other family. Nieces, nephews, her husband's family.

Her brother in Sagunto. She often spoke about him. They were very close even though he was quite a bit older. In fact, she was going to stay with him when she left. My own children often went with her to visit. They loved it on the farm.

Allegiance. The brother's allegiance.

How would I know, she says. He lamented the low wages of farmers, that's for sure. Then the restrictions on casual labour. Encarna told me it affected him badly, not being able to get day labourers from outside the province. Half the harvest went to waste because they couldn't pick all the fruit. So he wasn't happy about that, but I don't know if that amounts to allegiance or not.

No, the doctor deliberates. We can't say that.

She has nieces, María says. Her brother's girls. He had four daughters. Felipa died of tuberculosis quite a few years ago. Two of them were married but they went to the front right at the start. Encarna was very worried about them.

The doctor looks at her intently. Republican, he checks for

confirmation. Good. What group did they go with.

I don't think Encarna knew. She always got mixed up with the various factions. The FAI, the POUM, the CNT, the PC. Good girls they were. Hard-working. One of them was injured, last September, I think. She was in a sanatorium. La Casilla, if I'm not mistaken.

The doctor takes her hands. He has never done that before. That's good, María. This might help Encarna's cause.

Long live the Popular Army. A bitter wind pushes his greeting through the door as he comes in with Julita. Fina looks up, startled. He must be one of the militiamen Julita often speaks of. She has never mentioned this particular man before but her honeyed voice says everything. Ernesto this, Ernesto the other, Ernesto take a seat, Ernesto have a bowl of rice. As if they had surplus. What will María make of the visitor when she comes back.

Fina, could you turn down that racket. We have a guest. Julita's irritation is palpable. As if we understand French, anyway, she smiles at Ernesto.

The French racket is English but Fina doesn't correct her. The words she herself doesn't understand are in her head even as she lifts the needle off the record. Something she used to dance to in Paris when they went out in the evenings with the Americans. One of them in particular. The words had meaning when he sang them in her ear, moving slowly to his own hum. Many times he tried to explain the meaning but they always ended up laughing at his failure to explain and hers to understand. Still, the words stuck to the memories of those nights. Meaningless with a meaning regardless, she thinks, replacing the slate disc in its sleeve. Because there is meaning in a look and a touch, meaning in a confident movement, the pressure of an arm slipped around a waist.

Iudu sam tin tu mi
Sam tinde simpli misti faismi
tel mi guai sudi bi
iu jede paur tu jipno taismi

Lemi lif nidiur spel
iu dude vudu de iudu sobuel...

For iudu sam tin tu mi

De nobodi els cudu.

Did she tell Ernesto the house is not hers. Did she tell him to march around the kitchen instilling terror into elderly people and children with talk of an explosion at a metro station in Madrid. He won't say how he knows this, though he hints at access to privileged information. She doesn't recall reading about it. A blunder the government would rather keep quiet, perhaps, but it is a detail Julita ignores, beaming instead at the man. How easily we succumb to an air of authority. Should he be telling us this, Fina wonders.

Her father has nodded off. Good. He wouldn't like to hear this. Señora Rojas mumbles her mysteries, staring at Ernesto as if her prayers are directed to him.

Ernesto says the metro station was being used as a projectile and explosives factory. Wonderful, by Julita's estimation, how the government is making progress in this wretched business.

Hundreds of men and women working in it, Ernesto relays. Blown up. It's horrible, he says, proud that he can handle horror with appropriate stoicism. Fascist scum.

But I thought the rebels hadn't been able to get that far into the city, Fina says. Have they broken the Republican lines. That would be the beginning of the end. There has been nothing about it in the papers.

A blank stare. Then, No, no, of course not, my dear lady. They're nowhere near our lines. Still scurrying like rats up on the Guadarrama. You can hear them crying like babies at night. They know the game will be up very soon.

So the explosion had nothing to do with them, with the fascists, Fina tries to clarify.

This time there is censure in his silence. You should be careful, he says eventually. Anyone would think you're a fascist.

Fina is stunned at the accusation. I'm just trying to underst—

I'm only saying, he cuts her off, because I care about Julita. I wouldn't want anyone thinking she was consorting with rebel sympathisers.

Fina is one of us, Julita looks at Ernesto. Her smile is forced, as are her words. There are no rebel sympathisers here.

I can't see him but I know he's there—I can hear him

Ernesto—but he didn't have a name—didn't speak—just footsteps behind the wall

how did I get trapped here—where are the others—shit—where's Juanjo

how long this wait—hold your breath—hold your breath—he might leave

should I come out from behind the wall and surprise him—one bullet

but I can't move—can't move even when he sees me—he knows I'm here—petrified—I can hear his footsteps stop as he turns the corner—hunter locking onto the hunted

nozzle of his rifle raised—I can see it—he'll pull the trigger if I don't—his eyes molasses—something familiar about them

fear—him too—I smell it—but there is no time to think or see or feel

my shirt is drenched—pants soiled—we do things we never imagined

it's alright—clam down—I'm here—safe in my box—it's just that pompous know-it-all strutting in the kitchen

The rice she made for supper is gone. Alicia told her his name was Ernesto. He came with aunty but she knows nothing else. He just came.

Fina confirms. She doesn't mention Julita's sweet tones or his militaristic strides around the kitchen. No point stirring things up. The distress in María's face is already evident, although she is making an effort to play it down.

And what of it, Julita shrugs, blasé about her sister's confrontation.

María is furious but she mustn't let her concern betray him. That's nice, she says instead, you need company. I think there are a few oat biscuits in the cupboard. We can have those for supper.

Don Millán and Fina look at her, surprised. The children too. Such a fine line between insanity and magnanimity. Insanity and everything else.

Julita's spiteful mood has spilled into today. It's impossible to run a house with everyone sauntering down for breakfast at their leisure. What do you think this is. A hotel. She grits her teeth. I've just put away everything. She glares at Alicia and Tomás but turns to Manolo. I'm surprised at you.

In the crossfire, Manolo looks at his aunt. Pitiful, gentle, the boy expected to be the man, protector of his mother, defender of his fighting brothers. Stunted as he tries to fulfil roles unsuited to him. Will he ever be allowed to be who he really is, Fina wonders. She begins to understand why he is slow at his lessons. Turmoil on the inside. Is that what the war has done to him or would he be so quiet and faltering regardless.

I told them they could lie in because it's Sunday, María says.

You're hopeless, Julita hisses. Besides, Manolo is my son. If anyone is going to give him orders, it's me. I won't have you turn him into one of those feeble-minded, undisciplined rebels.

Everyone stares from one sister to the other. If they were alone she might hold her counsel but she can't let the children see her cower. Not anymore.

In case you haven't noticed, she says quietly, this is my house and you are my guest here. From now on there will be no fixed time for breakfast on Sunday. It is a day of leisure in this house.

She holds her breath. Maybe nothing will happen. Maybe Julita will back down.

You're gone in the head, you are, Julita scoffs. Unfit to be running a house. Children, sit down. Next time you're late for breakfast you can go without. Including Sundays.

Dumbstruck.

Her sister under rubble, crushed by debris. Her sister against a wall with a hole in her head. Mouth gaping. Eyes whitely heavenward. Blood from her mouth. Her sister frozen solid, fused to a frozen basket of bread. Her sister with the welts of wet gangrene like some of the militiamen. As little as a day, doctor García told them. Extremities but also internal organs. Her sister waxen in the bed. Natural causes. Her sister curled like a poisoned rat under the floorboards. In agony. Her sister in flames at the stove. Her sister with an axe stuck in her skull.

None of this will ever happen, of course.

For distraction Fina reads aloud. Oranges and mandarins to be sold only in the market and at a fixed price. Ninety cents a kilo. Well, at least it's a fixed price. Seventy-five thousand kilos of salted cod to be made available next weekend, available with your ration card for rice from 1937, not the one issued this year. But it has to be the ration ticket for week fifty.

We should still have those, Julita perks up.

Oh bother. It's only for certain shops in Barcelona, Fina reads on. My goodness, twenty years in a labour camp for a man accused of desertion. Antonio Fuster Richet. He said he had been given permission to go to Barcelona to say goodbye to his family but the military court didn't find in his favour.

Maybe that husband of yours deserted, Julita throws in.

Fina looks up at Julita, marvelling at her provocation, at the pettiness and half-truths she uses to build her sense of power. But María is deep in thought.

The pages rustle again. Dear me, Fina continues, it's hard to find anything cheerful in the newspaper. Oh, here we go. You can get five pesetas back if you return empty stock cube tins. We have some of those, don't we.

A third morning and she has not had the opportunity to empty his pot. Last night señora Rojas took a break from her endless mysteries to say something about a foul smell. No one else seemed to notice but María's heart skipped a beat. With every hour that passes her distress increases. She has the impression today of still trying to catch her breath.

It's freezing inside and out but she feels hot and there is now a distinct whiff. Public urinal. The unkempt corner of the park in the height of summer. What must it be like inside his box.

This one she rips up. The stove will swallow it whole and it will be gone. Poof.

Close to the end, you say. Too close. Blindly in the night they come at you. Sparks and the recoil. Less than human, you say. Savage. Like children playing at war. Echoes in the hills. Gunfire and their moaning and this is music to your ears. Wave after wave, you say, pushing forward. I can sense you scoffing at their attempts. They must be brave even though you say they are disorganised and demoralised.

But what is bravery. The aura of bravery around you the day you left. Now I think it was arrogance bolstered by the uniform, the shine of your boots, gleam of buttons. I bet they sparkle even as you inspect trenches, crunch mud and pine cones underfoot. Cleanliness next to godliness. I believed it too. Maybe the trenches have helped to reinforce your convictions whereas what I am living through here has shaken mine.

Discipline. Rectitude. Your favourite. Little of it here with the house overrun. Everything just happens whether I will it or not. Whether Julita pulls her many strings or not. Whether I pray to God, his mother, his saints. They have all deserted. The only one who can't desert is me. I am weary and your letter doesn't help. I see your black gloves, black boots, and I start shaking.

His birthday, Julita declares. He's their father, for goodness sake, even if he has abandoned them.

A lesson in how to torment children. Does she enjoy it. Was she always this mean. They look aghast at their aunt. Then at their mother.

Of course Papá hasn't abandoned you, María reassures. He would never do that. Her protective instinct is genuine even if the rest is pretence. Ramón would never abandon his children, she glares at her sister. The war will soon be over and he will come back. She smiles at the children but there's something missing.

What do you know about the war, Julita scoffs.

Keep the peace. At all costs, peace. She sighs. Well, it's a good idea, Julita. We'll have a party for him even if he's not here. The nineteenth. That's Friday, isn't it.

The moment she commits to this her energy evaporates. Exhausted, she excuses herself, at a loss as to how a party will be organised when they have nothing.

A damp patch on the ceiling is an interesting thing. In an uninteresting sort of way. Brimming with uninvited elements that make it sombre. Like age spots. When did that happen. She doesn't recall it being there last winter. Character that gradually turns to decay. It will flake off, eventually. It could peel away and fall on top of her, lying on the bed, unable to move. What if the ceiling fell on her. Crushed her dead. End it our father who art in heaven. Quick. Bloodless. Thy will undone.

Voices downstairs and she is startled to find damp patches on her cheeks. An indistinct buzz.

It's great to be alive, she hears don Millán. Is he talking to himself. Hardly. The voice seems to be coming from the bottom of the stairs. He must be talking to señora Rojas whose muttered mysteries are the most comforting sound in the house. Then rippling laughter from the children followed by something in French from Fina. Maybe they are immersed in one of their classes. All the voices louder and even Julita is laughing from the other side of the room. What could be so funny.

This is what it's like for him, she thinks. Fitting pieces of conversation together. Guessing at tasks from the direction of the voices. Except he is in darkness, unable to leave the box and she can do nothing. Even less today. Unable to move. She tries to raise her arm but can't. She could get away with it yesterday, saying she was feeling unwell, very tired, but doctor García detected no temperature or swollen glands. What's wrong with her. This numbness. She can't leave him unattended for another day.

The blanket slips down again and her face creases in disgust. That smell, she repeats to herself.

Now Fina gets it too.

Twitching noses scour the air. It's almost a competition. Who gets it. Who doesn't.

It's not my trousers, is it, don Millán whispers to Fina.

No, she whispers back. I'll wash them tomorrow, just in case, but I think it's señora Rojas. It seems to be coming from over there.

Well it's not something in the kitchen, Julita is adamant. I keep this place spotless. Doctor García says you could perform surgery on the kitchen table it's so clean. You must all be imagining it. I don't smell anything.

where is she—why upstairs so much—I will have to consider breaking out of here—tonight—and be damned with the consequences—I can't go on

Julita up before there's any need—scrubbing everything within reach—swish swish of the broom—more vigorous today—does señora Rojas not wake—there's nothing to sweep—is it me—does she sense my presence—positioning and repositioning chairs—then clickety click

this morning she keeps looking around—puzzled—it must be me

doctor García up soon after—complimentary of her cleanliness—better than any hospital he has ever been in he often says

you get it too she said but I heard nothing from him—was it me

Fina and her father whom Julita mostly ignores—from their conversation I can tell the doctor often attends to him before they come down—for privacy—surely María could find a moment to talk to him

stomach growling—three days with nothing even though I carefully rationed the rice—a man can live for weeks on an empty stomach—the body starts to consume itself

the others in dribs and drabs—always someone in the room—surely she could find a moment for a private word—unless she's very ill

We celebrate for ourselves. To show we have marked the occasion, acknowledged the other person. Not fallen into negligence or forget. Its opposite is grief, though grief, too, is for ourselves. Try grieving on your own in silence, she thinks, dragging herself downstairs.

French class has been all about paper balloons, colours, cutting and its implements, thread, lack of glue. And paper hats. *Joyeux Anniversaire*.

They will keep the balloons and hats as gifts for Papá when he returns from the war. *Des cadeaux*. Proof that they thought of him. *Je t'aime beaucoup, Papá*.

In Ramón's absence, doctor García jokingly said they should make a snowman to replace him at his party. *Le bonhomme de neige* sits seriously at the head of the table wearing one of the paper hats with a Spanish flag drawn on it.

He'll need a scarf, don Millán prompts. It's freezing in here.

Le bonhomme de neige is quickly kitted with one of Ramón's scarves. Don't worry, don Millán answers Tomás's concerns, it'll be a long time before he melts.

The doctor observes Julita take off her apron, grimace at the flag as she paints her lips.

Well, well, Ramón, you're finally back. Your wife misses you so much. It's one of those remarks that is just not funny even though Julita chuckles. She refuses to wear a paper hat. Silly things, she criticizes, even one with a flower and not a flag. Fina, on the other hand, obliges. Fina always self-contained, the doctor notes. There is warmth in this woman's heart. At the children's insistence, because they know she has treasures in her trunk, she has changed into a silk dress and a string of pearls. Is it possible a woman can look so alluring in a lopsided paper hat. Julita raises an eyebrow of disapproval, at the dress that looks more like an undergarment, and the way it clings to Fina's curves. Señora Rojas is her usual blanket shape on a chair with a paper hat on top. The children giggle and Julita glares.

María, he observes, takes her time coming down from bed to celebrate her husband's birthday. There is more to her sadness than his absence. I am letting her down, the doctor thinks, not for the first time. He must get to the bottom of it.

There is no cake. *Pas de gateau*. Bread with a spoonful of condensed milk is all they need, according to Julita, mostly because it was she who procured the condensed milk, with much fanfare, from the militias at the Communist building. So she told them, although everyone suspects Ernesto had something to do with it. Surely civilians can't just take provisions for the troops on a whim.

They sing happy birthday to the snowman, clap, call him Papá. The children find this hilarious but María looks pained, still not quite herself.

Noody, Alicia says in a fit of giggles that become contagious. Papá is in his noody, she repeats, almost rolling off the chair with the laughter. Don Millán smiles and shakes his head. The children are an endless source of entertainment.

Such a rude child, Julita mutters, stony-faced.

That man is as pale as a ghost, señora Rojas squints in the snowman's direction. Another fit of giggles. Let's check his heart, Tomás suggests, pulling out the stethoscope. Squeals of laughter now. Uncontrollable.

You'll make a fine doctor someday, doctor García smiles at Tomás, hiding his own concerns. María, he says, I think you should go back to bed now. Let me help you.

He is appalled. In his attempt to help his patients he has been responsible for a man's deteriorating health, this man she is hiding and refuses to name. From what she has confided, he will need medical attention. And even though she has not made the connection, he also knows he is responsible for her weariness, this failing humour that afflicts her.

Downstairs the gramophone belts a scratchy swing song, Fina calling out steps. Three, four, one. In that shimmering dress.

Redress the situation and little time, he thinks, aware of María staring, hopeful. We will have to wait until tonight, when everyone is in bed, he says. Will you be strong enough to go down and clean out under the stairs. I will move señora Rojas upstairs to my own room and keep watch. Distract the others, should they wake. You will have the kitchen to yourself.

She cannot speak. Tears of relief. He will respect her privacy for now. He understands that to name her own husband is to add a further layer of risk to him. Anonymity offers more protection.

Relief sabotaged by pain. By wasted muscle and petrified joints. His feet, dragging from one side of the kitchen to the other, are almost alien to him. Light, however dim, burns his retinas.

The deterioration is shocking but neither mentions it. She pulls out a chair for him but, No, he whispers, I want to go out.

Moon and stars eclipsed by clouds. He stares into the night, into new understandings of what it means to be alive. Icy, the air stings despite the doctor's heavy coat, hat, scarf, gloves. He fills his lungs. Big. And again.

Gunfire in the hills is making her anxious. You'll freeze to death. It's too cold.

I want the cold. Onward he trudges, mindless of sludge or potential soldiers, of the bottoms of his trousers soaked, sticking to his skin. That wind..., he marvels.

It's too dangerous out here, she tries to steady herself on uneven ground. Too wild. How can these few minutes feel like such an eternity.

I want the wild. I want the wind and the wet. María, he is already breathless, I can't tell you how good this feels. She holds him, shivering in the middle of the empty street, disquieted by the drone of planes overhead, alarmed at how her arms encompass his entire torso, his ribs through the wool.

Here, she says, pulling a hip flask from her pocket. The doctor said you might need this. But drink it quickly. We should go back indoors. Is he oblivious to the threats.

Good cognac. He smiles, savouring the blaze in his body. How can time stop in the taste of lips, the warmth of her breath on his neck.

Back inside, a tub of warm water and a bar of soap by the stove. A clean set of doctor García's clothes on the chair. This is unexpected. It takes both of them to peel off his icy clothes, lift his wasted legs over the side of the tub. Pain and he winces, clinging to her as an older man might, lowering himself into the tub.

Water moves back and forth in response to small movements of his leg. Warm, wondrous, he thinks, staring at water as if it contains the secret to life and death. One movement causes another. And what of sitting here now, alone with her. What will this cause. He closes his eyes. Feels the soap as she lathers his back. Then circular dreams on his shoulders, gently down his arms, across his chest. Bliss between his legs, hidden by suds her fingers along his thighs, unhurried over the summit of his knees.

Out of sight, the doctor keeps vigil at the top of the stairs. He hears the lap of water, their whispers, hears a sudden metallic CLANK, ricochet and SPLASH. The soap has flown out of her hand. Hears her gasp and the clatter of a broken spell. Shh, he hears him say.

The doctor holds his breath, looks around and instinctively down, into the kitchen. He hadn't intended to breach their privacy but so much noise. And now he can't unsee. Is it because of what the war has done to him or because… Deserted. He can't help staring at them. What has he let himself in for.

Some days nothing happens except sirens screaming outside. Nothing but this waiting for the war to run its course. Waiting, imagining the end. Nothing but thick mist blanking out the houses across the street. The future is like this. A blur. Nothing, screaming more nothing. And the present is a struggle to get through one kind of nothing so as to reach an unknown other nothing.

Sirens here because things happen elsewhere while nothing happens here. Fina has read more than once that Germany and Italy are not respecting the non-intervention agreement. They offer the rebels supplies.

How come Germany and Italy can breach it and other countries can't, Julita has often lamented. Do they not care.

Russia has no problem breaching it, María counters. He has told her about this under the stairs, where many of their supplies and support come from. Surely you know that, Julita. How do you think your comrades are getting their supplies.

You need your head examined, little sister. You've got it all wrong. I'm down at the Communist building every other day and I can tell you it's the decent people of Spain who are giving everything, absolutely everything to support the government. Even stuff they don't have. Every last scrap is donated. Not like the attitude here. I'm embarrassed to be living with…

With what. What are you embarrassed to be living with, Julita.

Go on. Say it. María is incensed. You have choices, Julita. You are welcome to leave if you find it so embarrassing to live here.

She wants to add more, that Julita invited herself here, that she was never wanted here, but checks herself at Manolo's stricken look. The alarm of conscience louder than the sirens outside. She wants to scream. She has never felt a greater urge. An urge to scream stronger than when she pushed these children out. That urge was nothing compared to this. She wants to scream DAMN IT JULITA, I WANT TO LOVE YOU. YOU'RE MY SISTER. WHEN DID THIS HAPPEN.

Julita takes a deep breath, so deep she feels she might burst, as if she had not been breathing properly for over a year, slowly strangled. Today, a letter from her middle boy Fernando. After almost a year at the front he has been given leave. Has the air in the kitchen really become lighter and the miserable flame in the stove less cold. Unable to stop smiling, she is expansive with everyone this morning. Fernando will be home in two weeks, they are told, one by one. Fernando is coming back.

Manolo's eyes light up. Two weeks, he says, echoing his mother's smile.

Yes, son, isn't that great news. Unable to stop smiling as Manolo spreads his arms, coming towards his mother, she reaches for him, too. I'm so happy, she squeezes him tight, tighter than either of them has ever hugged.

For the rest of the day, everyone wants to know about Fernando. They share their own stories about young people they know at the front. Relatives, friends, friends of friends. All day praise for the militias and the soldiers, the enormous sacrifices, their bravery. Surely the war will be over soon. The government wouldn't be giving leave if it didn't feel it had things under control. That's what it must mean. No doubt.

Happiness is infectious because they need it to be. Everyone is longing for something, trying not to think about it because thwarted plans are too disappointing.

Julita laughs. Listen to this. And, if you can, please cook your shoulder of lamb, she reads. No one does it like you, Mamá, and the slops we get here have turned my stomach to mulch. I'm not sure I'll ever recover. She shakes her head. What's he thinking of, she laughs. I've written to him about our conditions but he must think we're still living like we used to. Shoulder of lamb, indeed.

A long, hooded cape of emerald green brocade with fur trim. Down the front, glittering buttons with embroidered detailing at the eyelets. The lining on the underside shimmers a paler shade of green. Sumptuous patterns and texture.

The children gasp. Are you going to wear it, Alicia wants to know as Fina pulls the cape out of the trunk.

Goodness, no, Fina smiles. I was thinking I could—

Put it on, please, please, Alicia implores. Let's see what it's like on you.

Is it yours, Tomás asks. They have never seen anything like it. Where did you get it.

Oh, someone gave it to me, I don't remember, Fina shrugs, throwing the cape around her shoulders. I used to wear it in Paris, she says, rummaging for her gloves. Like this, to stay warm in the evenings when I went to restaurants. I had a hat, but I don't know where... Maybe it's in the other trunk. She stands, wrapped in the cape, filling in the idea of a hat with her arm above her head.

You look like a princess, Tomás says in awe.

You're so beautiful, Alicia sighs.

Fina laughs, taking off the cape. Do you know what I'm going to do with it, she whispers to them excitedly, looking at Manolo. I'm going to trade it in town for a shoulder of lamb.

Crestfallen. They cannot express it but it seems wrong to part with the most lavish thing they have ever seen. Rich greens and sparkling buttons and exotic fur in stark contrast with everything in the house. This touch of splendour that transforms their Fina into a goddess.

No, Alicia breaks the silence at last. Don't trade it.

Fina is taken aback. Dear Alicia, she says, crouching to her level, there's no point keeping it and I would like to repay your mother and your aunt in some small way for all their kindness. Besides, your cousin Fernando hasn't had proper food in a very long time. He deserves a treat.

No. I don't want you to trade it, Alicia sulks. I want you to wear it.

Oh dear, I shouldn't have said anything. Fina looks up at Manolo but he avoids her gaze. I thought the three of you would be dying to have a delicious dinner with Fernando. Look, when the war is over, she tells Alicia, I'll get another cape, you'll see. There'll be lots of these capes. Nicer ones.

Alicia looks at her, not entirely convinced. Do you promise. Exactly the same as this one.

Yes. I promise, Fina assures. Now don't think about it anymore. And please don't mention it when Fernando is here. She squeezes Manolo's arm fondly. We're going to give Fernando a proper welcome home.

The battle of Teruel. The army of Aragón. It is mentioned in every paper the doctor brings home. That's us, Tomás is mildly amused.

Us indeed. Run. RUN.

Two hundred planes in twenty-four hours today. Non-stop drone and throttle swoop. Señora Rojas is dragged every time under the table with the women. If she is afraid, she shows no sign of it, admiring Julita's cardigan. Don Millán stays on his chair by the stove. He is too stiff to hunker under the table but he has the pan Fina gave him for his head. Better than nothing. The children run into the linen cupboard and Alicia is crying. Tomás puts his arm around her.

Shells explode and the sticky tape on the windows just isn't enough. Shards fly. Everyone huddled under the table gasps. Every muscle contracts.

So much for the victory that was announced, María throws an angry look at Julita. This is far from—

Another explosion. Tighter together they huddle. Chairs arranged around the table like something resembling the housey game the children play, as a barrier against flying debris. But this was not what housey was ever meant to be.

Are you alright, Julita calls as quietly as she can to the linen cupboard. A shout might bring the house down.

Nothing.

Manolo. Answer me.

Yes, Mamá. Alicia is scared. She doesn't like the dark.

Alicia, don't be afraid, her mother whispers as loudly as she can. Tomás, are you looking after your sister. This will be over soon and we can all come out. Can you hear me, Tomás.

I'm hungry, Mamá.

Stay there. Don't you dare come out. We'll have food very soon. Just a little longer. This will be over very soon.

Sous le pont, d'Avignon, on y danse on y danse... Very quietly, Fina starts to sing.

Christ, Julita mutters. How can anyone think of food or start singing in the middle of this.

Come on, Manolo, Fina urges. Sing with me.

The planes scream overhead. They will kill lives and hope and joy. Sisterhood and brotherhood. The town will be obliterated one of these days but Manolo's sweet tenor voice filters through. And right now, right here, that's the only thing in the world that counts. *Sous la table, de Teruel, on y tremble on y tremble.*

Fina smiles. He will survive, she thinks, as the song gains momentum for no one knows how long. *On y tremble tous en rond.*

Good man, Manolo. *Sous la table, de Teruel, on y—*

if there was a direct hit it would all be over—I wish

but then again

Fernando—in a few days—he must have changed—poor lad—
what he must be going through—and now he's coming to this

Encarna is on her mind and now this ad in the newspaper. How much is a life worth. Is one life more valuable than another. The doctor has no leads so far. Maybe she could use the money Encarna gave her.

What do you think, she whispers tonight, sitting beside him at the table.

He never really knew Encarna but that's not the point. He knows her well enough in the way María speaks of her, in the taste of a hardboiled egg, in the enthusiasm she inspired in the children for their Christmas play. He knows her as a hard-working woman whose bar kept the town spirits up well into the war. Not easy. A woman who always got on with living, who extended kindness. The men are busy destroying the country, he thinks. The women are busy trying to hold it together.

Yes, he says with a heavy heart, you must do everything you can. It's a good idea to use the money for that. But where will you find a phone.

That's it then. Hair. Rouge. Her good hat pin. I need to get out, she tells them. Polished shoes.

Julita shakes her head, still sweeping fallen plaster and shards of glass several days after the aerial bombardment. They must find a large plank of wood for the broken window. For now, they have given up their pillows to shore the hole.

Apart from the fact that you'll get pneumonia if you go out like that, it's dangerous out there, she admonishes María.

It doesn't seem to bother you when you go to the Communist building.

That's different. I have protection there and a purpose. Julita is indignant in her own defence.

Is that so. Protection that goes by the name of Ernesto, I suppose.

That shut her up. Glorious silence from Julita. María smiles, comparing it to the din in the distance now. Cavalry, she heard someone say. Republican tanks against rebel horses. Twisted times, godforsaken, but there are silver linings. The snow has begun to melt. She hasn't been this far from the house in weeks.

She has to look twice to make sure this is Joselito's bar. Every building on this side of the street is unrecognisable. Shells of buildings and empty shells strewn on the ground. There is no door, no sign saying *Bar Joselito* over what used to be the door. The end wall is completely blown out and the upstairs floor, unsupported, has slid down almost in one piece. It lies at an angle over the hole that used to be a wall, making a neat triangle. Glass grinds underfoot and rubble shifts but she's in. Seeing the bar destroyed like this is almost as distressing as if a loved one had died. Dust and debris everywhere. What are the chances the phone line survived. As she expected, none.

Possibilities run out. Or is it just her inability to think of alternatives. The only option left is a risk but she can think of nowhere else. It's amazing that the Communist building is still intact. Franco's rebels have been focused on the convent and the town square.

So this is where Julita spends her time. She can think of no excuse for being there if anyone asks but she is not in control of her feet. She could be flotsam floating through the door, into the hum of people in and out of rooms.

Looking for my sister, Julita Vázquez de Morla, she hears herself answer the question. Where did that come from. Yes, Antonio's widow, she smiles uneasily.

The woman brightens, suddenly more open. I haven't seen Julita today, but she might be in the supplies room. End of the corridor, down the stairs, second door on the left.

María tries to look confident, as if she belongs. Left and right she glances into rooms, their doors open to a sense of purpose. Brave efforts, as in many other similar hubs around the country, to make life easier for the soldiers at the front. She imagines Julita here, enterprising, respected among her comrades. By the time she reaches the stairs her heart is pounding. Then she sees the room, empty and in semi-darkness, shutters closed. She sees the desk and on the desk the telephone. Her feet move cautiously towards it and words from her childhood fill her head. Biblical words she never understood before. *For we wrestle not against flesh and blood, but against principalities, against powers, against the rulers of the darkness of this world.*

One as bad as the other, she marvels, retrieving the slip of paper from her pocket. Quickly looks around and dials.

84915. Can I help you.

Fina's disappearance with Manolo fills the morning. Despite Julita's repeated huffs of exasperation about their whereabouts, no one says a word. Tomás and Alicia have been sworn to secrecy. The mission must be a surprise.

It's dangerous out there, Julita frets. And I want Manolo to chop the last of the wood so it will be ready when Fernando comes.

Agnus Dei, Lamb of God, señora Rojas sings in a shaky voice, *miserere nobis.*

Julita stops stomping about the kitchen to stare at señora Rojas. No one has ever heard her sing before.

Agnus Dei, she continues fervently. The children glare at her, afraid their aunt will make the loose connection with lamb.

Under Julita's puzzled look, don Millán shrugs. Don't worry about them, he says. They probably went back to what's left of the old house for something.

She doesn't like not knowing what's going on. Neither does she like the children's conspiratorial smile at don Millán. And where on earth did your mother go dressed to the nines, she snaps.

it's hard to hear don Millán tell them stories—not something I ever did—how will my children remember me

laughter—it's a welcome distraction even for me—something soothing about the old man's voice rising and falling—bringing the characters alive

what did I do—certainly none of that—why not

practical things—the olives at harvest time—buy them roast chestnuts by the town hall in winter—a treat—maybe they'll remember that—mostly I was tired when I came in from the fields

now I wish I had spent more time with them—I would like them to have known me better—so they will have good memories to look back on—someone to look up to in the future—but I dare not think of the future

Where did you get this, Julita is stunned. The butcher never has anything these days.

Manolo smiles at Fina, proudly placing the side of lamb on the table.

He gave me a mix of dried herbs to flavour it, Fina says. His wife has surplus, apparently. Chopped rosemary, thyme, mint, wild garlic leaves. It smells divine. She offers the open cloth to Julita to smell and the aroma fills the kitchen. It takes so little to be transported to life before deprivation. Summer and its abundance. Forgotten scents. I taught his children in the Liceo, Fina explains. We can keep it frozen until Fernando arrives.

And parcheesi, Manolo adds. I always wanted that. He said his children are gone and don't use it anymore. Alicia, Tomás, parcheesi, he calls, running to his cousins.

Parcheesi, indeed, Julita sounds miffed. I need you to chop the remaining chairs, she calls after him.

She stares at the lamb. Fina is not a woman she could ever warm to. Not a woman with a head on her shoulders, flitting around as she does in fanciful garments, with the foreign nonsense she calls education, flinging her legs in the air and jumping around. Useless, all of it. Sleazy.

How did you pay for it, she asks.

Is there a touch of reproach in her voice. It takes Fina a moment to reply. Good quality material, she explains. His wife will be able to use it or make a fine dress.

Always had a streak of vanity in her, Julita thinks, remembering the butcher's wife. Mutton dressed as lamb. Hmm..., she examines the meat. Well, thank you, Fina. It's very thoughtful of you. It will make a great meal for Fernando's homecoming, she adds with a smile.

Unsafe, angled precariously. Jostling back and forth, they brave the steps. Up. Not yet, Manolo steps back down. Slowly. Slowly. Fina climbs beside her, for reassurance. No, you won't fall now, Fina says. You are like the Queen of Sheba. Exactly how royalty travelled in bygone times. Señora Rojas says nothing, stares into space, wide-eyed.

In the morning, the entire process in reverse. Wide-eyed, into space she stares. Nothing, says señora Rojas, and no one hears her. Exactly like the Queen of Sheba, says Fina. Like royalty. You won't fall. But it's no reassurance. Beside her, Fina descends, slowly, slowly. Back steps Manolo, bravely jostling up, down, to the side until they reach the first step. The basket lands with a thud.

This is absurd but the doctor has his reasons, no doubt. Up at night, down by day. Warmer for señora Rojas in his own room, he claims. He can keep an eye on her during the night.

She was happy downstairs. She had privacy. But no one is arrogant enough to contradict the doctor. Now Manolo and Tomás have to carry her, perform this evening ordeal and it is mortifying. The blanket slips. The boys are shocked at her legs, blue veins in knots round her shins, skeletal arms, flaps of skin and a faint whiff. Afraid she might snap from the pressure of awkward angles as she balances on their arms. Downstairs the others share the embarrassment and discomfort. When Tomás misses his footing everyone's foot jerks.

It's too hard, Manolo moans after days of this. I could try making a hoist with a pulley. Like the one we saw at the fair. Do you remember, Tomasito.

Clever lad, don Millán is impressed. I'd have you work with me in my workshop if I still had it. There might be some tools there that you can use, rope and spools with hooks, if the place hasn't been raided. It would have to be a double pulley, but I have a feeling... He shakes his head. Still, you might get ideas if you go to the workshop. Will you take them there tomorrow, Fina.

Another display of power from the front. Fantasies neatly scripted. Drawing room order that makes no sense.

I am everything but a woman to you. Was I ever anything else. A punching bag. Now you treat me like a child with this nonsense. Who do you think you are writing to. Enemy tanks trundling towards you and you dismount, unperturbed, swirl your horse by the legs over your head like a lasso, hurl it at the tanks. Pegasus, you write, flying with fearful whinnying and the reds dropped their weapons in terror and ran. The reds gathering their body parts. Reds trampled under horse hooves, pleading for mercy. Reds drowning in their own red bl... and you run out of ink. Resume, retracing the word blood so it looks like a blotch.

Why can't you just admit you've seen no action. I wouldn't be surprised if there was more action in this room than wherever you are. Such overblown rubbish you come up with. Makes you feel powerful, I suppose. That's all that matters to you. Oh, I can see right through you now. Yes I can. I'm ready for you now, you miserable coward. Brute. Excuse for a man.

Tonight they choose under the stairs. For privacy, even though they trust the doctor keeping guard on the landing.

So the doctor has decided not to push it, he whispers.

Apparently, she says. It's strange, given that he was so insistent on your need for medical attention at first, but now he seems to think that I can probably judge the state of your health without his intervention, that the exercise around the kitchen and more regular food should be enough. You will need to build up your strength if you are to leave here. He'll help us with that.

I'm glad. He's discreet. He probably prefers not to know who's hiding here. And he's right, I feel so much better already. We will get through this, my love. Come closer. I need you.

I am here. Right beside you.

I will do anything for you, you know that. Even if it means giving myself up.

Don't say that. She frowns in distress, puts her finger to his lips. But I do know it.

Soft, her fingers as he kisses them. I would. Especially, if…

Shh… I know. Another letter came. He sounds crazier than ever, telling ridiculous stories as if he thinks I might believe them. We'll be gone from here with any luck before he comes back. Where will we go, she asks, snuggling closer.

LA VANGUARDIA

Barcelona	DAILY AT THE SERVICE OF DEMOCRACY	15 cents
Year LVII. – No. 23,046	Offices: Pelayo 28 Telephone: 14135	Saturday 22 January, 1938

Enemy Pressure on Teruel Front

New Assault and New Losses

No change to our lines

OFFICIAL COMMUNIQUÉ

Ground forces:

EASTERN FRONT—-The bloody battle at Teruel continues. Rebel troops advanced aggressively but have been contained and forced to retreat without any serious breach to our position. Rebel aircraft carried out intense attacks all day, bombing and machine gunning our positions. Our troops relentlessly outmanoeuvred the fascist positions with punishing counterattacks.

He squints so much now when he reads, even with the candle right up to the page. It's the same every time, he laments. How well they're doing, how important it is to save this town or that town, to gain a bit of ground here, a building there. When it's lost, wait till you see. They'll dismiss it as not being so important after all.

When is Fernando coming, he asks eagerly. What a gem Fina is, getting the meat. Does that hole magnify things or is there really enough to feed an army. It looks substantial.

It is, she nods excitedly. I can't wait to see him. He should be here in a week.

Encarna is an old woman. She has known for many years that age is a number but she never thought much about how circumstance could compound the number. A box 50 centimetres wide and 40 centimetres deep compounds the number. Lack of sleep. Pain. Torchlight like the sun in her eyes, burning day and night through the slit in the box. The ticking clock.

Getting pulled out after several days is small relief. There is still pain. She cannot stand or think. Crumples to the ground and is hauled by militiamen up the stairs she came down an eternity ago. What now. Dropped on a chair in the cloister. Sack of coal. Pain is how you know you are alive.

Why is she being told this person knows her. She has never seen this person but a man claiming to be this person stands before her. He talks and her muscles scream. Her head pounds with the infernal tick tock that is never switched off in the box. He is looking at her, trying in some way not to look, and she is vaguely aware of a left breast sagging through her open robe. No strength. It will have to stay like that, bared for all to see. Decency was part of who she used to be but she is no longer even a woman. Barely human now.

This person talks and she shivers. He talks while he stands and approaches. Now he will strike, though his tone is kinder than the others. The infinite twists of terror. He will pin her down the way the others did. Is he talking about money. Why when they already took it all. Talking he comes, stretches out his arm and she hasn't got the energy to raise hers in defence. Talking he pulls the robe across her. Gently. Talking he covers her bare breast, steps back, makes a reverential gesture like people did when she was a woman.

Out of here. Did he say that. Did he say María. She wants to respond to this but it might put María in danger. Knowing someone can be fatal. As fatal as knowing no one.

The cloister grows black, starting from the delicate columns and their Doric capitals. The evening light narrows, narrows. Black engulfs the fountain till it disappears. The path narrows, narrows to a dot of light. She slumps forward, fringed in black, and falls. Out of here. Oblivion is bliss and it is pitch velvet black.

Mamá, what does ESTE NUMERO HA SIDO VISADO POR LA CENSURA mean.

It means just that, says Julita. The censor reads every edition of the newspaper to make sure we are getting the right news.

Do other newspapers give the wrong news.

Certainly they do. The fascists only have wrong news in their papers. Boastful things. Lying propaganda. They want everyone to believe that they are winning the war. That's all they write about.

How can they say that if it's not true.

They say whatever they like to make themselves feel good.

And who is the censor.

I don't know, son. A man who knows about what's correct and what isn't, I suppose.

Do the fascists not have a censor so they don't get wrong news.

Who knows. But even if they do, he'd probably let them print the lies they want to hear. Did you get everything you need for your contraption.

You mean the hoist for señora Rojas.

Yes, the hoist.

No. It's too complicated. Don Millán says we'd need to drill into the walls and the ceiling, and they might fall down. He says the best solution is to have señora Rojas move downstairs again.

Red-faced from the chill and exertion through snow with a heavy bag, Julita pulls off her gloves, finger by finger.

The letter she takes out of her pocket looks official but María's name is on the envelope. What's this, she asks. The postman himself was wondering.

Official, they all know, means bad tidings. No one utters a word but Manolo walks over to his aunt and links arms with her.

María smiles at him, kisses his forehead.

They steel themselves as she reads in silence, leaning into her nephew.

What is it, Mamá.

It's about Encarna. María reads quickly through the letter again, aloud this time. A detective I employed.

When did you do this, Julita asks. It's a criticism more than a question.

María ignores her, says nothing about having called the detective from the Communist building. She continues reading. Followed her trail to a convent…led to believe she was being held there but no one could confirm this…because of privileged connections was given access to a woman he was told was Encarna but she looked nothing like the woman I had described… inclined to believe the woman was not Encarna…neither corpulent nor garrulous and the names of family and friends didn't seem to register… my search, I regret to inform, has been inconclusive to date… can continue enquiring in the south, perhaps, other detention centres and hospitals, but this will require more time and appropriate remuneration.

Oh dear. What do I do now, she asks, turning to the wall in dismay.

You should have told me about this, Julita shakes her head. I could have got Ernesto to help. He would know what happened.

Slowly, she pulls from the bag a jug of liquid milk, tins of condensed milk, coffee, sugar, dark chocolate, a kilo of flour, a bottle of sherry. I'll make a cake for Fernando, she smiles at her audience. In case there's not enough meat to go round.

Their eyes linger on the supplies. What was María saying. Oh yes. The neighbour who disappeared.

Sleep. That's all Fernando wants. A clean bed that will feel as if he is sinking into a cloud.

No parcheesi, not now. He tousles Manolo's hair. You've changed Manolín, he says. Are you taller than me.

They stand back to back. Manolo wins, squeals Alicia, clapping her hands.

I'll arm wrestle you, Manolo challenges with caution. His brother looks so weary and thin.

Fernando shakes his head, starts to cough. Later, Manolito, he catches his breath. I'm too tired. You've no idea.

María and Julita give up the bed. They will camp in the kitchen. She has anticipated this and left food for three days under the stairs. Even so, it's always a worry. Will it be enough. Will he make noise.

What is it, Julita asks, seeing Fernando's hesitation at the clean sheets and the hot bricks to warm the bed.

I thought I'd never see you again. He is almost embarrassed to reveal his thoughts. Or Manolito. Sometimes I have nightmares that you've all disappeared, José too, like Papá, and I can't find you.

In her arms he's her little boy again. Not the soldier she expected. For a moment, it frightens her. His letters are always so cheerful. Where is the Fernando who left for the war, brimming with energy and enthusiasm. And he hasn't stopped coughing since he came back.

Come on, get into bed, she says. You need a good rest.

Now that he's back he feels different. Everyone in the house looks on him with pride, treats him with a respect he never remembered receiving, as if he is grown up now. But on the inside he is in turmoil. Like a child who has woken abruptly from a nightmare.

Don Millán speaks to him like an adult. He used to have family in Segovia and knows the area where Fernando is stationed. Manolo is beaming, as if Fernando lends him status among the cousins.

Look, Manolo tells him.

Fernando nods with a big smile, unable to speak through a coughing fit.

We're going to try it out this evening, Tomás adds. But we have to fix it up first.

A wicker basket. This is what they found in don Millán's abandoned workshop. Tomás beats the dust off it. Alicia lines it with the cushion Encarna gave them for their nativity play.

Some of the wicker is undoing here, Fernando remarks when he catches his breath. I can patch it up for you. A few strips off the dried palm branch will do the trick.

Co-operation, that's what I like to see, don Millán nods in satisfaction. I used to carry firewood in it, he reminisces. It'll be perfect. And you got Habibi's reins. Brilliant. Ah, Habibi... He was a good horse. Now we must hope señora Rojas obliges. She should fit.

They are praising the soldiers as he savours the lamb. Praising the efforts of the Republic to keep them well fed and armed in the trenches. They don't know, he thinks, and I can't tell them I haven't seen the sun in a year. That I've been living in a cloud of smoke and dust. I can tell them nothing about the food. About anything.

Tell us, son, you who are at the front, are we winning the war, his mother asks and her encouraging tone suggests there is only one answer.

The lamb is really delicious, even better than he remembered. He savours its delicate garlic flavours and the juices from the meat soaked up by fresh, crusty bread. He looks at his mother, remembering the brigade leaders deliberately taunting them with roast lamb, eating it slowly in front of them while they were starving. He can't get enough of it now.

Don Millán laughs. Let the boy eat in peace. He's waited a long time for a decent meal.

Fernando grins, nodding with his mouth full.

Well, son, she probes again, as he wipes his mouth, tell us.

He didn't expect to be feted like this. Nothing is what he expected, even though his mother had explained their living conditions in her letters. But, somehow, he imagined being at home. Not in his aunt's house, a hero to these strangers. He can't tell them he lives every day in the knowledge that his life is worth less than a gnat's. He tries to gauge what these strangers and his mother want to hear.

A drink of water to calm the tickle building in his throat. We're definitely winning, he tries to sound confident, as manly as he can. He has such a lovely smile, María thinks. The image of his father. If our bullets don't finish them off, Fernando continues, sooner or later our farts will. You've no idea what beans do to a regiment.

The doctor is impressed. Needs must, he says, holding señora Rojas under the arms while María helps lift her legs into the basket.

But why... Where... the old lady is quite confused. Am I going home. The world tilts at a hostile angle and is she really being bundled into a basket.

Don't worry, señora Rojas, this will make it easier to get upstairs, the doctor assures her.

Ay-ay-ay..., she shrieks, folding into the basket. Ay-ay-ay..., as the ground begins to move.

There is anticipation in the room. Hopeful smiles, Julita linking arms with Fernando.

Is that comfy, Alicia asks, patting the pillow behind señora Rojas's back. She gets a panicked look in return.

Manolo and Tomás each pull on the reins. Up the stairs they go.

Ay-ay-ay.

The doctor pushes from behind. Strong lads, he encourages, as the climb begins. It is smoother than they expected.

Genius, Julita says, looking at Fernando. What do you think of your brother's work.

Manolito, you're not just taller than me, you're cleverer, he shouts up to his brother. You too, Tomás. Pull. You're nearly there.

Señora Rojas's breathing is shallow. I'm going to fall, she complains, clinging to the sides of the basket.

I'm right behind you, the doctor reassures. Don't worry, you can't fall out.

Bravo, boys, don Millán calls out. The simple solutions are always the best.

Exhilaration at the top of the stairs. Applause. Alicia hopping up and down. She looks at her brother with pride. Everyone rushes upstairs to welcome señora Rojas to the landing, as if she had been travelling for days.

I can't stop looking at him through the hole—plagued with guilt

is it bravery keeps him going—although he is so much younger than me—fear perhaps—even though he is clearly unwell

no one will say it to him but he looks older than his years—eyes sunken—legs like sticks—waxen face

I have been a coward—I never thought I would feel it so intensely—it's killing me

I should be on the other side of the wall

will I see him again—and José—will I ever get out of here

I should be at the front—but...

I should be anywhere but here—reduced to nothing—what's the point of this—what will the children think of me if they ever find out

Even when quiet has descended, the house is never quiet. Doctor García is aware of everyone's breathing, everyone's footsteps, wood and metal creaking, shell fire in the hills and aircraft hum. For hours the infernal quiet keeps him awake since María asked for his help. If only things were black and white like the soldier pinned under the girder, fire spreading. That was an easy decision. The small saw he found and the soldier's frantic nods. Tie a tourniquet and to the task. The quicker the better. The quicker the better. The quicker the better. The quicker the better. Through the bone. Done. Done. Done. He dragged the man out of the burning building with seconds to spare. Marvels that he cannot recall a single sound.

Hospitals are not safe, he told María a few days ago. How would she know. It is to our discredit, indeed, but the militias trawl them regularly. I've seen them drag wounded men out of their beds and take them away. For a little walk. But there's an English chap with one of the medical units who might be persuaded. Quite a character but a competent fellow. He's built nothing short of a mobile hospital inside a truck. He has everything in there. Refrigeration for medication and blood, sterilizers, bunks. One sees so much courage, bloody-mindedness.

He cannot read her look. What do you think, he asks. This Englishman, he is idealistic too, like so many of the foreigners. They don't quite understand the many threads of what's happening here—who does—but their hearts are in the right place. I have spoken to him about such things before. I am sure he will agree. But I won't ask unless it's what you want.

Papers, yes, not so difficult to procure. Is he really offering to arrange for forged papers too. This was not what he had in mind when he asked her for refuge. He must think of it as a practical decision.

They want the parcheesi to last longer than all the other times they've played because this is the last one. Leave is over and time contracts.

They watch Fernando walk down the street, his backpack slung over his shoulder. Bulging compared to when he arrived. Food his mother insisted on packing, a cough mixture the doctor gave him and tobacco from the butts Manolo collected. Smartly he walks. No point dragging it out.

He can hear their goodbyes. Head high, he thinks. Give them confidence. In him. In the Republic. At the corner, he turns around. Their breath is hovering in the February air. If only I had a picture of them now, he thinks, already nostalgic. Furiously they wave, as if the strength of it might carry him through the next few months. It will have to. His mother's handkerchief, white, dabbing her eyes. Farewell, but not surrender.

I think you're in love with Fina, he teased Manolo in the bedroom this morning. He never saw his brother blush before. They laughed and he prodded Manolo affectionately until it became a pillow fight. He looks at the group, tries to fix each face in his mind, remembering the last time he saw his father. That's what war does. Nothing for granted.

He pushes the thought aside and waves more vigorously. Adiós, he shouts. I'll be back soon.

Adióoos, Fernando, adióooooos. Kisses, big wide blowy love to last forever. Write to us. Adiós. Loud. As loud as they can shout.

Adiós, he waves and waves. Keeps waving, looking back, waving as he walks out of sight.

Why were you at the Communist building, Julita demands to know.

Why does the room start floating.

Was it Ernesto. Is that it. Are you spying on my private life.

What. No. I don't give two hoots about your private life.

Of course you don't. You never did. So what were you doing there.

Nothing. The room stops spinning and María anchors herself to a chair. I needed a phone. To call the man who is looking for Encarna.

What is it about the particular blankness of a disbelieving face. Not snooping around for information about Ernesto, then, Julita mocks as if she has outwitted her sister.

No, María protests. I've just told you. I needed a ph—

Well, Ernesto asked me to marry him, if you must know.

None of them has ever heard a more dispassionate declaration. She said nothing while Fernando was here. Somehow, congratulations feel wrong.

And will you.

I'm thinking about it.

No one notices the colour drain from Manolo's cheeks.

pounding in my ears

does this mean she might bring that man—Ernesto—here more often

one thing after another

why is my whole body rigid—pain in my back—buttocks—shoulders—head—is there any bit of me that doesn't hurt

the sooner María arranges my escape the better

it's worse having seen Fernando again—watching him leave

what are his chances now

painful to hear him telling them about it—choosing his words carefully—joking—a positive picture for them—no one wants to really know—his mother wouldn't have let him go back

The road is deserted. Partly because the locals know but must pretend not to.

Encarna sits with men and women in the bench at the back of the truck. A small flicker of hope that they might be released and it will all be over. That man's words back at the cheka, *out of here*, ring in her head, but she hardly remembers any of what he said in the cloister. Mostly, a cold premonition fixes each person in place. Like a stone in the stomach. If they move too much it might cause havoc. She heard in Santa Ursula what happens in the backs of trucks like these. Bloodied ropes under the bench give credence to the stories. Or is that just fear running wild.

The truck stops. She has been brought here in one of many trucks, just as she was taken to Santa Ursula. No one ever explained why or why here now. Little point in asking, though one of the men is muttering, They're going to kill us. Some of the women seem to be murdering prayers. She remembers that day outside Joselito's bar. Before it all began. The Hunchback walking into the square. It was swift for those men. Knees, ground, head.

They must take off their flimsy robes. Men and women shiver, naked, but fully clothed in their solidarity, staring at the ground to preserve each other's dignity. There is a humanity in it that is comforting.

Three men at the edge of the pit, shovels in hand. She is pushed forward with the men and women, some too weak or wounded to walk. Some fall, are picked up, flung into the pit. Surely not alive.

Her head fills with thoughts of Joselito. Nine years. She is glad he never saw what has become of his beloved Spain. Glad she never brought children into this hell. Who'd have thought their grief back then could culminate in this moment of intense relief. Things work out, he used to say. And true, this is the proof of it. Maybe she will see him soon. She clings to the idea, unaware that she is smiling.

Lined up with the others at the edge of the pit, the shots begin. Here goes. Except this time it's not the Hunchback and his Falangists. It's men she thought were on her side, their shots deafening along the line and her eyes are squeezed tight, streaming, streaming, and the thud of body after body tumbling into the pit and the cries of men and women protesting and the sudden silence and the oh most sacred heart of oh most sacred sacred heart most oh most sac—

No *Gaceta* today, Papá. Paper runs out like everything else. Things they never thought of as luxuries. We're lucky the doctor can bring it to us so frequently.

Don Millán doesn't seem to mind. His mood is good this morning, pain or no pain. The whole world is in conflict, he sighs, and we haven't a clue what's really going on. I don't think the young lad told us the full story of what's happening. He probably doesn't know. We can only sit here and hope someone breaks that non-intervention agreement so this diabolical business can come to a conclusion. I don't see any other way. I think it was my trousers.

What. She looks at him quizzically.

He leans over to her. Some things are not meant for other ears in the room. The smell, he whispers. It's gone.

It takes a moment to register. Oh, Papá, were you really worried about that. She recalls his recent sadness. Could it have been triggered by such a small thing. I don't think it was your trousers but, yes, now that you mention it, the smell is gone.

Clear sky tonight and María worries about being seen. But his mind is elsewhere.

Be very careful with that man Julita brought over the other day, he says.

Ernesto.

Yes. I saw him. He is deeply committed to the Communist cause but his commitment is unquestioning. Misinformed, I'd say. I've seen much of that. The kind of man who doggedly defends one small part of a principle even when the larger reality doesn't make sense. And he relishes power. I could see it the way he strutted around that day. Puffed up peacock.

But she has stopped listening to him, trying instead to understand the flashes in the sky. It's not unusual for the sky to flicker and flare at night but this is different. Usually, flashes in the night are accompanied by the rattle of engines stalling, then agonising silence as they spiral through the darkness, plummeting. They hold their breath always for the man in the cockpit. Republican or Nationalist doesn't come into it, though mostly he says, Polikarpov. They know that despite the newspaper reports it is the Nationalists who are gaining control of the skies.

You can tell the Russian polikarpovs because they sound like you, he says, when you whisk eggs. Putt putt putt putt. Slightly faster, but not much.

Are you comparing me to a fighter plane, she laughs.

Believe me, there's more fight in you than in those planes. He tightens his arm around her waist. Some of them are as flimsy as cardboard. He must be exaggerating. The Junker 52s, on the other hand, the German planes that the Nationalists have, they drone like an angry bee. I've seen those too and they're impressive. Sophisticated machines.

But tonight there are no planes, only a startling luminosity they have never seen before. Everywhere peacock shades are fanning the sky. Mesmerised, they watch wavering green and turquoise, swathes of amber, ribbons of maroon. Giant brushstrokes that keep painting new patterns.

María blesses herself. Good God, what's that. If it wasn't so beautiful I'd think it was the end of the world.

I don't know, he frowns. Maybe it's a fire.

It couldn't be. I've never seen the sky swirl like that. Those colours rising from nowhere. Maybe it's the enemy.

Which enemy.

Let's go inside, she says, just in case.

Still, it's hard not to get drawn into the bright colours, the expanse of it. Magical. We are like rabbits stunned by hunting lamps, he thinks. Maybe rabbits feel wonder more than fear.

Even though the cards depend on chance, the faces concentrate every evening as if there were some probability to winning or losing. It's the concentration that matters. To remind them of what sanity was like, the way things were, as long as the shelling isn't too loud.

What did you say, son.

Are you getting married, Manolo repeats under his breath.

Maybe, Julita replies. When the war is over.

The numbers on the cards blur in his hand.

Rummy, she declares cheerfully. Would that be so bad, son. We would have someone to take care of us. A nice house in Tarragona, where Ernesto is from, with a room to yourself so you can sleep uninterrupted.

Is it bedtime, señora Rojas asks from under her blanket. I only just got up.

I loved your Papá, Julita continues, but… You must never think I didn't love him, do you hear me. But Papá is… When the war is over we will need to rebuild our lives. Tell you what, son, I will invite Ernesto for dinner some evening and you can—

You will not.

Did she really say that. All eyes turn to María. She must have said it. She hopes they can't sense the extent of her alarm.

Were it not for him, Julita almost spits, we'd still be living on your insipid broth. Where do you think all this comes from, she points to the cups of coffee and chocolate on the table. You owe him a lot. All of you.

We owe him nothing, María is trembling. She must steady herself. Besides… Besides what. Think of something. Besides, it's too soon. For Manolo. For all of us.

I will decide when it's too soon and when it isn't. Julita's voice is rising. You've never had a practical bone in your body.

Ladies, please. Don Millán lays his cards on the table and stands. He winces in pain, stretches awkwardly. We're all a bit overwrought. It must be time for bed. Maybe one of these evenings the children could do another concert for us. Wouldn't that be nice.

Even with wood boarding up the window the kitchen cools too fast at night. I wish everything was different, María sighs. What could we have done to make things different, to live some other life.

Nothing, he whispers. We're together now, aren't we. Despite everything that has happened. This is more than we could have hoped for. What are you smiling at.

Nothing. I'm just enjoying watching you eat. I love you. She kisses the top of his head. I love your gentleness, I love your words, I love your bravery and resilience. He scoffs. I'm happy you can get out of the box and eat proper food at the table, even if we have to be vigilant.

He is thinking something he cannot express. Something about her. Something he can only transmit in silence, as if he is reading her innermost thoughts, sharing his.

Botifarra, he suddenly breaks out of a trance. I haven't had it in years. That reminds me. I was thinking about Ernesto.

Julita's...

Yes. Maybe you should invite him over. It will make things easier for you if she's encouraged to pursue that romance.

María is surprised. Will it not just complicate things.

He shakes his head in resignation. As if they could be any more complicated than they already are.

And what about Manolo, she asks. He will never forgive me. Maybe he will never forgive his mother.

He suddenly looks overwhelmed by the weight of the predicament. Close to tears. María squeezes his arm. We are all victims of this war. So much of what happens and even our own decisions are out of our control, driven by the need to survive. We have limited choices. Choices that are not choices at all. Choose to fight at the front or be taken out and shot for not fighting. Nothing is logical or normal anymore. People are forced to live and behave like animals. No one can really be blamed for what they do.

I adore you, my love, he whispers. You know you mean the world to me. He sighs. My heart aches for Manolo but a happy Julita is preferable to an unhappy Julita. Invite him over.

Are you sure. It seems so wrong.

She'll be happy.

no effort—not even polished his boots—and he calls himself a military man—not the right man for her

I can't bear to think of him as a father figure for Manolo

the boy so defeated—he only brightens up when he sings those songs with Fina—daft I would have said in the past but everything looks different from in here—distilled to some pure nub of things that is easily overlooked in real life out there

she's an unusual woman—not one I would have had much respect for before but she brings something essential to the house—a lightness that carries weight

gobbling the food while he talks about how far the rebels are being pushed back—hogging attention—did I do that—talk of suppressing other Republican groups for going about things the wrong way—if you didn't know any better you'd think he was one of the fascists

I never noticed before how women wait on men—servile—fussing—they do it with the doctor too—did I look so smug and satisfied when they waited on me

what is it about people who talk too much—suck all your energy—María looks drained and everyone else is bored one minute—irritated the next—but he doesn't see it

No, I never married, Fina replies.

You must be a rubbish cook, Ernesto chuckles. Only Julita laughs with him. Don Millán throws him a cold glare.

Fina wants to say that she could never love just one person. That would be like chopping off her arms and legs. She wants to say she prefers to be free to love whomever she wants in whatever way she wants. For the sake of love and not to fulfil anyone's expectation of love. The way she loved the American because he missed everything back home so much that she became his home. And the young teacher because his eyes were blacker than the night and his words and his body penetrated deeper than the night. Only slower. Much, much slower. And she became his word-studded night. And the dancer because she was so strong on the outside yet a cloud on the inside, vaporous, blown asunder by any wind. And she became her wings and taught her to fly. And the rich American lady who liked boats and champagne because she had never known anything else but was always searching for everything she had never known. In people. In houses. In paintings. In love. And Fina became her vision of what it might be like if everything was stripped away. Exiles. The nakedness of these people she loved, for whom home was anyone who was willing to understand the myriad ways a heart and body can be cleaved. There is little room for marriage and its singular devotion in that, but it's not something she can explain to Ernesto. She can't even explain it to her father.

I never felt any need to marry, she says instead.

Ernesto looks at Julita as if she owes him an explanation for this strange assortment of people.

Is it really so hard to understand.

Conversation switches to the war. To the citizens of Madrid who refuse to leave the city.

They are unpatriotic, Ernesto criticises, hampering military operations.

It's not easy to leave your home, Fina says, but Ernesto won't hear of it.

It's a matter of duty, he insists, for any Spaniard who considers himself anti-fascist to obey that evacuation order. But no. Hard-headed as they come, clinging to their little bits and pieces. They're probably members of the anarchist groups or the General Workers' Union. Always causing trouble. Doing everything their own way. They should be dragged out by force if they won't leave under the government's protection. They're making it easier for the fascists to gain ground around the city. Nothing more than imbeciles.

Who is he insulting.

Mind your language. There are ladies present, don Millán calls for civility.

Manolo's stomach tightens. He needs to get away from the table. On impulse, he stands, wondering what to do next. The empty soup dish on the table catches his eye so he carries it to the sink. Away.

Sit down, man, Ernesto calls after him. She'll do it, he says, nodding towards Alicia. I always say the kitchen is no place for a man. How come you haven't brought him down to headquarters for training, he asks Julita. He's old enough.

Does he not know her two older sons are at the front and her husband is dead. He's not sixteen yet, she tries to defend Manolo. He'll go when—

He should be training. We need all the help we can get. You know some of the boys are fifteen, some as young as fourteen. This young lad should have joined them long ago. We must look into this, Julita.

False cheer suddenly brightens Julita's face. You could find out for us if Ramón... Where...

Damn. What on earth possessed her.

Ernesto flashes a look at María. Your husband, he asks. What division was he with.

Stupid mean bitter twisted bitch. She knows he was called to the Nationalist side. Has she actually told Ernesto. Is she completely crazy.

I... I don't remember, María stutters, oblivious to her sister's apologetic glance.

Don't you write to him at the front. Does he not write to you. The questions come with a mixture of surprise and admonition. It's the one thing that keeps the men going, news from home, apart from the supplies we send.

Yes, yes of course I write, María answers, trying to sound calm. We haven't had word in a while. But don't go to any trouble, please, she says as sweetly as she can manage. You are clearly very busy. Besides, no news is good news. I'm sure he will get leave when it's due. He is needed at the front.

Does he believe this prattling. How long are they going to sit here digging their own graves.

I'll make enquiries, he says, and she fears she will faint.

Shut up, will you. Just shut up, she shouts at Julita when he's gone.

I didn't mean to, honestly. The words were out of my mouth before I knew it. I didn't—

I said SHUT UP.

She doesn't want to shout at her sister but she can't help herself now. Bile from somewhere deep in her gut. You're evil is what you are, she screams. EVIL.

Now she is responsible for the distress on Manolo's face. He has never looked so helpless. He will crumple, implode and never recover and it will be her fault. She, his favourite aunt, shouting at his mother like that. Oh, Manolo, sweetheart, I'm sorry. I'm so sorry.

Raging, she runs up the stairs, fleeing from herself, wondering with each thumping step what he is making of all this under the stairs.

the world is crumbling—every thought twisted—every word misunderstood—everyone suspect—it's my fault for suggesting she encourage Julita to invite him here

it would have been better to put up with injustice and hardship of the old kind than go through all this—if they had known what it would be like how many would have chosen to steer us towards war

hell cannot be worse

brutes—all of us—brutes—that's what the war is doing to us—even my beloved María is succumbing to the poison—how can anything ever return to normal—how will we ever forgive ourselves

A story, they agree in the dark. Something to throw Ernesto off the scent. A regiment for him to search through. By the time Ernesto finds out Ramón is nowhere to be found, he'll have escaped.

I'll get Julita to ask him, she nods. What regiment should I say.

A moment is all he needs to think about it. Fifth Army Corps, eleventh division, he answers.

How so sure.

It was one of the Brunete divisions, he says. There were so many losses that many men must be unaccounted for. It will be plausible not to find someone in that division.

She has never thought of the comfort of a plan. The focus it brings. Something to cling to and work towards. The more she thinks about this plan, the calmer she feels. Dead men quietly sinking into the earth, unclaimed. Strange to think the dead were never part of any plan, yet now they come, rotting, to her rescue, Ramón hiding among them.

The room is swimming again as she opens the envelope. But this latest letter surprises her, shakes her in a different way.

It's hard to tell these days what is real, what is madness, what is important, what isn't. The world has done an about flip and we are all standing on our heads trying to convince ourselves this is normal.

Ludicrous stories. Last time it was supernatural horses, today it's football with the anarchists because they're bored with losing the war. As if they'd send you formal invitations to play football in the middle of war. In these freezing temperatures. And you win, of course.

Get to know them so you can outwit them, you say. Play them at their own game, then catch them by surprise. Everything is strategy with you. Is it ever possible to truly know someone. I thought I knew you, once. Your words, your kisses, walks we went on, so long ago, and you would pick wild flowers for me and tell me about trees and butterflies, the secret language of birds. How you would protect me from the dangers of the world. I thought I loved you then. But I was too simple. Too trusting.

Days slip by, indistinguishable. Monotony in forgettable variations. Which is why they look forward to the doctor's return in the evenings, always late but cheerful. Deserving of ritual. Julita takes coat, hat, scarf, gloves. Fina, the newspaper. María starts serving a single plate. The children hover while he greets everyone, enquires after señora Rojas. Already upstairs in bed, transported in her basket like a queen.

Alicia, please, her mother complains, putting bread on the table. Not now. The doctor is tired and he needs to eat.

At Alicia's dismay he winks. Never too tired for a medical consultation with my colleagues, he says. The stethoscope dangling around her neck bounces back to life. You should check my heart rate, Doctor Alicia. I'm colder than usual tonight. You might find my heart is beating faster.

Pulse, seventy-seven. She checks in her notebook against another day's pulse, hops up and down. Yes, faster, but nothing to worry about.

Well, that's a relief, the doctor says. Sometimes I think I'm dead on my feet. María smiles. We've had more casualties than usual at the hospital today. That's what kept me, he begins, and they take a seat around the table. This is what makes the humdrum of every day a little more bearable. The doctor's stories. Vivid and grotesque and humbling. About heroes who save lives. Their ingenuity in restricted conditions, and it is balm of sorts.

He pulls out a flask and pours for don Millán. Scotch, he says.

Would you believe one of the internationals told me he uses it for shaving. Not this one, of course, he clarifies with a grin. This one ended up unclaimed after we moved the hospital across to the school. Every time we have to move, things go unclaimed. Watches, flasks, letters, photographs, clothes, rosary beads, medals. It's hard to keep all the personal items together.

Don Millán raises his glass. To whomever it belonged, he toasts. It has become habit with the doctor's whiskies and brandies to acknowledge people he never knew. It seems only right. Water of life, he thinks. The colour of a good harvest.

Ah, this wretched war, the doctor laments, turning the whiskey in his tumbler. How is the pain today, don Millán.

Could be worse, don Millán sighs. Could be worse.

Cloud cover gives some sense of safety out in the open. Because of the freezing temperatures, their heads and faces covered with scarves won't attract attention.

We are fortunate, he inhales deeply.

The slush is making her stockings wet and fortunate is not a word she would use. I've been dying to tell you, she says, the doctor is working on your escape. Apparently, there are wounded soldiers sent to Zaragoza every day. He knows of a special truck that would be safe. Run by an Englishman he trusts. It might be possible to get you out of here. To Zaragoza or Barcelona. Maybe Valencia. Until it's safe to come back.

Come back, he raises an eyebrow in alarm. There'll be no mercy for a deserter regardless of who wins. Don't think I haven't been thinking about this long and hard. If I leave, there's no coming back. You must promise me, María, please, promise you'll join me, won't you. Wherever I end up. You and the children. I won't go anywhere without you. Please promise me.

the best option she keeps saying—best option—her voice distant so smiling—we will be together

but where—when

in the playground she replies—where we always play

María a girl the day I first went to her house

she pulls back the curtains and peers out the window—her back to me—skirt rising up her legs

summer dazzling—smell the jacaranda she says—but I can't smell it—tricks of summer—are you tricking me María

smiling and her words are the best option—only option—and summer beckons on the other side—three two one here I come— I'm going to find you

shutters wide and I run—to smell the jacaranda—to catch her— touch her—María—run to the window ready to fly through it— out—into summer—to find her

and suddenly the wall—hard I knock against the wall—gasp— wake

did I gasp in my sleep—hold my breath—hold—hold

María hears it. Alarmed, she shifts in the chair as clumsily as she can, clears her throat.

What was that, don Millán sits up startled.

Hmm, Fina looks up from her book.

I thought I heard something. By the stairs. A thud.

I didn't hear anything. You were nodding off, Papá. Maybe you had a little dream.

It was probably me kicking the leg of the table by accident, María says, trying to sound casual. Goodness, is that the time.

Come on, Papá, I'll help you upstairs. Fina takes his arm. Everyone else is gone to bed and it's getting cold. Besides, she whispers, we're keeping María up.

No, not at all, María fusses, scraping the chair on the tiles. Did you put the brick in the bed.

Yes, Fina looks at her kindly. Such a sadness in María's eyes always. It's hard not to feel she and her father are imposing but their hostess is so gracious about it.

Good idea, don Millán grins, bedtime is my favourite part of the day. Goodnight, María. I don't know where we'd be without your generosity. I will miss you all, especially the children, when this is over.

Don't worry, don Millán, we won't let you go far. The children

will still want you to tell them stories when the war is over.
They're very fond of you.

Cooking for much of Sunday morning. The aroma of fried peppers and onions, slow rabbit stew, and no complaint about Alicia being late for breakfast.

You haven't invited him back, I hope, María is suddenly concerned.

No. I just wanted us to have a delicious Sunday lunch, like old times. We don't have all the ingredients but— Julita stops, glances at her sister, continues stirring. He's searching hard for Ramón, she says to the stew, barely audible. In the regiment you told me to tell him. I hate lying to him and having to go along with the farce. It's very…

There is nothing to say. She watches Julita stir her guilt into the pot. War embodied in a woman at a simple task. The complexities it creates. It was of her own making, María thinks. Helping to solve the problem is the least she can do.

It smells delicious, she says.

I know that as things are, this is a lot to ask, Julita resumes, regaining composure, but it will seem very strange if I never invite him back again. He wants to tell you himself of his efforts.

Children, will you set the table, please. María turns to the others. Somber, their faces. Don Millán, Fina, señora Rojas, constant spectators to her life. They quickly avert their eyes, pretend they had never stopped reading, filing a nail. She is suddenly struck by how sick she is of these faces. Sick of illness, sick of snow, sick of being confined to the house and its secrets. Sick of reasoning and accommodating everyone. Talking is an effort, especially this conversation. I don't feel well, she says. I need to lie down, but please enjoy the beautiful meal aunty has made. Leave some for me for later.

He will relish it, she thinks.

There are people who work well, precision so fine not even the most astute authorities can tell. The doctor doesn't know who they are. Invisible, she thinks. How many people are invisible, working undetected, living underground. Is it for the money. The doctor has used the word clandestine more than once. A veiled word so she understands why he distances himself from invisible people. He doesn't know who they are, doesn't want to know, but he knows people who know people who know who they are.

He hands her their work without a smile. A document with official looking stamps and the name Guillermo Valverde Badía written in beautiful handwriting. Where do people learn to write like that. And a birth date she doesn't recognise. A new nationality too.

Chilean, she asks, alarmed. Is that not dangerous. I heard that several foreign families in Madrid were… In the early days… She doesn't want to appear critical of the government, not to the doctor, but news of foreign diplomats killed by Republicans was widespread.

He has a better chance if he's not Spanish, the doctor explains. Never mind that they're slaughtering one another, but the view now is that international conflict is best avoided. It's no guarantee, of course, but I believe it gives him some advantage.

Her eyes, fixed on the doctor, turn to the document in her hand. So much she doesn't understand. From now on, this is who he is, then. Guillermo Valverde Badía.

Was this a real person, she asks, or is it a completely invented identity.

For the first time the doctor sees something in her that he hadn't observed before. Practical, she is that, but there's a fragility, a sensitivity that could create unnecessary obstacles.

Does it matter, he tries to assure her. The main thing is it's his ticket out of here. That's the only thing you need to think of, María.

The idea of choice changes everything even if choices are limited. Now inside the box they are freer, feel less confined.

Words, warm in her ear, soft like his skin, and smooth. The most ordinary skin in the world, pale from this fading life. Faint smell of fear and desire. The wiry hairs on his chest. We are dying, she thinks, as he kisses her. Kisses starkly alive in the dark, their gaping need intense. She wants to cry. I want your tongue, she whispers, and gently he gives it. The moment of skin and lips and never wanting to stop. His vulnerability and resilience, all of it she wants.

I love you, he says. I have always loved you. Even before I used to come to your parents' house courting…

Shh… She puts her finger to his lips. I just want to be with you, feel every bit of you. You will be leaving soon. Who knows when we'll…

Don't think of that. He presses closer, brushing her cheek with the palm of his hand. It's just you and me now, and it will be in the future. You must believe that.

I want to.

So do I, he says, finding her in the dark, parts of her she has no words for and, close, their bodies forget, cling to this sensory world that is so familiar, so dangerously new.

From the bedroom she hears the door open downstairs. Hears Julita greeting and Ernesto's voice invades the room.

In the mirror she hardly recognizes herself. A permanent frown on her brow and is that a grey hair. She plucks it out. Rouge. That might help.

Manolo is on his mat at the end of the bed, writing to his brothers. He pushes aside the pages and curls up foetal as Ernesto's voice slinks under the door.

Are you staying here. Quietly, she bends down to stroke his head, that copious mass of curls that give him innocent charm.

Can I, he asks. I'm not hungry. I have an upset stomach.

Of course you can, she says. I'll keep some rice pudding for you for later. I'll try and get rid of him early. I have a pain in my stomach too.

A hint of a smile on Manolo's lips but he turns his head to the floor. Standing again, she faces the door. What did Fina tell them, before a performance, to steady the nerves. Blow big with her lips to relax the face. Silly noise, like a horse. Force a smile. It lifts the mood even if you don't think so. You just have to go along with it in the beginning. That's it, lips up at the corner. Surprising, what some people can teach you. Breathing, too. Deep in, slow out.

Why is life so complicated.

Pacing about the kitchen, as if his feet need to be constantly in motion. Could he be nervous, she wonders, coming down the stairs. Don Millán and Fina look strained through their politeness. Not their favourite person either, and it gives her confidence.

Julita took her advice and has made a simple meal. Let him not think they live lavishly.

Where's Manolo, Julita asks.

He's not well. He asked to be excused. Her firm tone is a surprise even to her, changing in the next sentence to charming. Ernesto, why don't you take the doctor's seat at the head of the table. He rarely makes it in time for supper.

It's easier than she expected once she eases into the role.

You must miss your family in Tarragona. Isn't that where you're from.

If his reason for coming to dinner was to talk about his search for Ramón, he has been distracted by his own voice, complaining about the syndicates and the workers' parties. They're hell bent on revolution, he says, dismissing fresh air with the back of his hand, as if the air is their obstinacy. They want to put the cart before the horse and refuse to follow orders. They're imbeciles, he scoffs.

Don Millán takes a sharp intake of breath.

Julita puts the rice pudding on the table. She has said little throughout the meal, waiting as anxiously as María for Ernesto to bring up the subject, and it almost makes María laugh were it not so nerve-wracking.

In his stride now, he tells them about the efficiency of the Communist Party, with a smile in Julita's direction. When we win the war, he says, tucking into the rice pudding, it won't be any thanks to the General Workers' Union or any of the others. It will be because of our discipline and strategy. Our military superiority. We must win the war first. Then we can think of revolution.

She can't stand it any longer. Now, she thinks. Get it over with. Her voice cuts through Ernesto's. I fear my husband may have fallen in combat, she says. He may be in one of the hospitals.

You will hear from your husband soon, I'm sure. Ernesto's response is decisive. In the same breath he turns to Julita again. I thought my mother's rice pudding was the best but this one may well rival it.

María is stunned, glad to be distracted by the bowl of pudding Julita offers her. Is that it, then. Has he nothing to say about Ramón.

Your neighbour, on the other hand, Ernesto picks up, Julita was telling me about her.

No one dares ask what exactly Julita has been telling him. María swallows a lump in her throat. Feels clammy. Maybe it's the cold. Fina's trick, she thinks, and again smiles sweetly.

Our lovely neighbour, Encarna. Yes, she disappeared the day everyone was offered safe passage out of town.

So I heard, he nods. I've been making enquiries. If I was a betting man I'd say it was the militias.

They look at him in surprise. Is he not a militiaman himself. No one asks for clarification. He must mean some other militias. From the factions he has complained about throughout the meal.

They're always on the lookout for bourgeois elements, he continues. Not that I disagree with them, but they should be focusing on the war.

Bourgeois, María exclaims. What has that got to do with Encarna. She could hardly be considered—

I'm just saying, he is speaking bluntly now, she had a business, did good trade from what I hear. I was never in the bar myself. I came to Teruel after it closed but you worked there, didn't you.

Why do his questions always sound so loaded.

I wouldn't say she was rich, if that's what you mean, María manages to say. Or bourgeois. Far from it.

Ernesto takes off again, about communal values, shared wealth, people getting ahead of others. It's not the Republican spirit, he says with a sense of finality.

She thinks of him under the stairs, Guillermo Valverde Badía, and is filled unexpectedly with hope. If she hadn't hidden him, the idea of leaving Spain might never have entered her head. But hearing Ernesto now, she knows that is exactly what she wants to do. Leave Spain. She can't help grinning, feeling sudden relief. We will leave. We will leave these crazy militias with their irrational squabbles and their warped ideas to fight it out amongst themselves. There is no one and nothing for me here.

Rude, arrogant, she thinks, looking at Ernesto through her new smile. Julita deserves him. The two of them can revel in their ignorance.

I have every confidence in you, Ernesto, she interrupts him, whatever he was saying. In you and in the Popular Army. We will win the war, she adds, to everyone's astonishment. She looks at them individually, but especially at Fina, in gratitude for the strength she gives her. It's getting late now, but before Ernesto leaves I would like to propose a toast to the Popular Army, she says, raising her glass of water.

I don't think I've laughed much since I got into this box but those final remarks of María's nearly made me splutter

he fell for it too—of course he did

now I almost feel sorry for Julita—does she not see that he masks his failings with an air of authority—that he has no real authority—that his weakness makes him so easy to manipulate with a bit of flattery or with the illusion of authority—makes him dangerous too

she is bossy—irritating—but I never realised she was so blind to human nature

poor Manolo—I hope María can persuade him to come with them when she joins me

There's a mobile unit leaving the hospital for Valencia on Monday. The Englishman the doctor spoke of operates it. He'll get you there. Other countries are evacuating their citizens on ships from Valencia. It's a safer option than trying to get you into France.

The sea. He has never seen the sea. That endless expanse that swallows people whole. He only ever heard once of someone who went to Argentina. They never came back. Where am I to go, he wonders, thinking of his new nationality.

It's hard to imagine distances. But far is always dark. Darker even than this box. He thinks of the bottom of the ocean, murky, the darkness of holding your breath, not knowing if you'll ever reach the surface for air. The distress of water.

She can't understand why he is objecting to this chance of escape. The doctor has gone to much trouble, at some risk, to arrange it.

I will go to Chile with the children as soon as I can, or wherever you are, she tries to reassure him. Manolo, too, yes. He might be persuaded if the alternative is having Ernesto as a stepfather. There's nothing here for any of us. Even if the town could be rebuilt it would never be the same. Nothing will ever be the same.

They fall silent, trying to imagine the future, and draw a blank they fill with platitudes.

maybe there's something in it—the fact that they'll take me to Valencia

maybe Uribe will watch out for me if I go there—summon angels and saints to protect me—calm the terrors of the sea in my head

I remember being embarrassed when he spoke about it—terrifying and wondrous I imagine it with its three-headed monsters and sirens—embarrassed to admit to him I had never seen something as simple as the sea

I will think of Uribe—his good cheer—the paella he promised when all this was over

just a few more nights—then I will be Guillermo Valverde Badía

it scares me—but I can't tell her that

How is it possible for simple instructions to be such a burden. He can already see the muzzle pointed at him if anything goes wrong.

A dressing to bandage his head. But first a razor blade. The doctor has thought of everything. Blood from the hairline under the bandage will be more convincing. Why did she never think to ask the doctor for a razor blade when they needed one.

Remember, just before dawn. Monday. While it's still dark. Walk to the end of the street. There'll be no one about. But he's not so sure. There are degrees of darkness and those who want to see things will see, even in the dark.

The medical unit will be waiting. He's to whistle. He can't remember the last time he whistled. Will he know how. The English doctor will be expecting him. And away. That simple. In Valencia, present his papers to the Chilean consul. Guillermo Valverde Badía. Seek asylum in the consulate. The Chileans have been getting many people out. Valparaíso. Home and dry.

Home, and a lump gets caught in his throat. How casually they once thought of home, its simple comforts and certainties. A place where they belonged. There will never be such a thing again. They will be scattered like leaves, always tumbling towards an unfamiliar place. Who will they be then.

How long is one minute, an hour, a night. He has known the
illusion of time since he entered the box but he will never get used
to it. Emptiness stretches time, and endless time undoes the spirit.
He would not have endured without María. When he tells her,
more earnestly than he has ever told her anything, she brushes it
aside. In these final days she wants no sentimentality.

I can't bear it, she says. I don't want to even think about it. You
gone. What might happen. I just want to be with you.

It is why they are still under the stairs when the pounding starts
at the door.

No one ever calls at this hour. Louder. They hear the floorboards
creak upstairs. The doctor, surely, will open the door before
everyone wakes up. His footsteps on the stairs. Urgent descent.
Thumps that sound like they will break each slat of wood and
come crashing down on top of them.

What is it, Doctor. Now Julita's voice, apprehensive at the top of
the stairs. Who can it be at this hour.

Through the wall they hear the voices at the door. The first is
young, male, looking for the man of the house. I am the man of
the house, the doctor says. I am Doctor Julián García. And who
are you.

A different voice, pushing through, requesting they sit down.

What's going on, they hear Julita's alarm.

Sit down.

You can't just barge in like this, the doctor protests. What do you want.

It won't take long, the new voice says. Just sit there and don't move.

Thumping over their heads, up the stairs. They must be wearing boots.

A scream. Fina. Mumbling from the children and her heart is racing, every muscle contracted to a point of pain. Banging of wood on wood. Is the furniture being flung around. Everything reverberates inside the box. She never realised the wall was so flimsy.

What are you doing here, they hear the doctor ask, but there is no answer.

Glass shatters. Crashing from upstairs. Men shout orders to look here, look there. For what, no one knows. Are they looking for her. For him.

Downstairs the thumping feet retreat and now they hear the kitchen being ripped apart. Cupboard doors opened. Pots, pans, clanking. Drawers grating on the runners. They can't be looking for people in the kitchen cupboards. Something else, then. It's small comfort. Whatever it is, the intruders finally give up.

Maybe it was minutes. Maybe hours. The men leave without another word.

Julita is the first to break the silence, sobbing with relief. I thought they were coming for Manolo. No one replies. Maybe the doctor has put his arm around her to console her.

I'm here, Mamá, they hear Manolo say. They daren't move to look through the crack in the wall.

Mamá, a tentative call at the top of the stairs. It is Alicia. Mamá, she calls again.

Where is she, Julita asks through ragged breaths. Are they all looking around now, wondering where María is. She closes her eyes and swallows, squeezing his hand.

Your mother went out for a walk, the doctor says. Let me take you back to bed, Alicia. Julita, I suggest you go back to bed too. Try and get some rest. We'll clear up the mess in the morning.

A walk, they hear Julita's incredulity. On her own, in the middle of the night. Doctor, my sister is completely mad. We should go out and find her. It's not safe out there.

She needed to clear her head, they hear him say. I am monitoring the situation, Julita. Nothing to worry about.

Calmly, he seems to be leading Julita upstairs again, pounding above their heads, explaining that María had a headache, that the children need Julita's reassurance now so that they can go back to sleep. The militiamen made a mistake. It happens. Wrong house. Nothing to worry about anymore. Clearly there was nothing here that they were looking for. It was all a mistake.

No point turning the doorknob so carefully to avoid making noise. The bedroom is in disarray, light bulb on, and they are all awake. Alicia disengages from the comfort of Julita's arm and runs to her mother, throws her arms around her waist. The boys sit more upright on their mats at the end of the bed and Julita glares at María. Everyone starts talking at the same time. Accusing, perplexed, whimpering, whining, outraged. In the onslaught she notices she is standing on one of the baby's cardigans that was thrown on the floor. Thank goodness the letters aren't here.

Mamá. So scared. Where on earth. Crazy. Clear your head indeed. Broken the mirror. Clothes pulled out of the wardrobe. And chairs. Broken drawer. Poor Tomás, foot bleeding. Stood on glass. Mamá. Looking for. No one knows what. Shouting. Banging. Crashing. Money, perhaps. Maybe that was it. Wrong house the doctor says. Mistake. But who. And where on earth.

It takes a while for the voices to settle. She remains silent through the avalanche of words. Bends to retrieve the cardigan and folds it lovingly, as if it contains the body of a child.

It must have been awful for you, she sympathizes eventually, rubbing the fibers between her fingers.

You've no idea. Julita is vexed. I'm going to report this to Ernesto.

The knots in María's stomach tighten. The very person on their lips under the stairs but she can say nothing to dissuade her sister.

No one has slept.

Splinters of wood. Shards of glass. Surprising the corners they get into. How monumental the task looks. How long to pick up things, shake them out, wipe down, fold, sweep. To reassemble a sense of place, or self.

There's no doubt, they thoroughly dismantled the house, don Millán states the obvious from his chair by the stove.

Still shaken and exhausted, María and Fina are clearing the last of the mess when Julita arrives back. Despicable, she tells them. He says it's despicable and he is going to look into it. They will be punished, whoever they are.

María's heart quickens. Has he no idea, she asks.

How would he, Julita exclaims. Why would anyone be raiding this house.

I just thought...

Julita stares at her sister. What did you think, she asks, as if she knows the answer will make no sense.

It's just, after he mentioned Encarna, I thought that maybe... Maybe he thought I had money here. Maybe he told some—

Are you crazy, Julita defends. Ernesto would never do that. He knows how we live, what we have and don't have. He had nothing to do with this. Honestly, you're missing a few screws, María.

Maybe he… Could it have something to do with Ramón.

Ramón, Julita repeats in disbelief. Why is her sister always so irritating, so illogical. What, she scoffs, you think they're looking for Ramón in the wardrobes and the kitchen drawers and under the beds. For the love of God, María. He has been looking for Ramón in that regiment you told me to tell him about. Why on earth would he be looking for…

Mid-sentence she stops. Lips part, just a fraction. Something she has never considered. Ramón. Her eyes open wide. Ramón, she asks, as if she never heard of him before.

Without looking at them, María feels the faces fixed on her and her sister. The silent spectacle of her life baffling this little audience, and now something unspoken has filled the room. It's as if they can read her thoughts, see right into her head and they know. María blinks, tries to breathe calmly, slow her heart, her head.

no—dear God—no—why did she put that idea in Julita's head

when she comes to me tonight I will try to get out of here—hide somewhere else—tonight and tomorrow—I feel so exposed now—surely the doctor can hide me for two more nights

stay calm—a million thoughts racing in my head—calm

they will come back—they won't give up on whatever they were looking for—probably the money—unless his search has roused his suspicion

stay calm—maybe it has nothing to do with Ernesto

most likely it's the money—they all knew about it—María told them the day the letter arrived from that man who was searching for Encarna—maybe it's that man—maybe he thinks there is more—that she is hiding money somewhere—maybe one of them told someone who told someone who

but they wouldn't—that would put them all in danger—who then

Don't worry, the doctor tells her when she expresses his concern. They won't be back. Under the stairs is the safest place for him until Monday morning.

He will give me clothes for you, she tells him later, for the journey. Tomorrow night, the last night. Everything is in place now.

Neither of them wants to think about it too much. The parting. The uncertainty. The added anxiety of the recent raid.

It will work out, she says because despite herself, she needs to hear what she knows may not be true. How many untruths keep us going, she wonders, thinking of the way the papers boost the Popular Army's morale, the way he has told her.

Yes. Yes, it will work out. I will send word when I get to wherever I end up, Chile, and you will—

I will, she squeezes his hand. I'll come and join you. She smiles, almost believing it will be easy. I'll join you with the children and we'll start a new life away from everything and everyone. We will find work in Chile. We will have a good life and the children will have a future. Chile must be beautiful. I think it has mountains. It will be just like home.

Why does none of it sound true.

I adore you, he says, holding her as tightly as he can.

Ernesto. Sweetly, Julita greets him at the door but they all hear the surprise in her voice. It's not because he has called over on a Sunday. It's the three militiamen flanking him, two with mallets over their shoulders. A casual threat. Come in, Julita greets him but it is only the habit of politeness. Even she is hesitating. Everything about the men, especially their silence, is an affront to politeness.

Ernesto whispers in her ear, pulling her in by the waist too tightly. For his comrades, perhaps. Or her sister and the others. A quarrelsome look in his eyes. There is shock on Julita's face but they can't tell whether it's at the words he has whispered or his boorish manner.

María wants to ask what's going on, what brings them here. She wants to tell the children to go outside but she mustn't. Anything she says might betray her. Go outside, she says. Is something wrong, she asks.

The way he looks at her she feels she might wither. Stay, he says to the children with a biting gentleness that falls colder than the snow. Slowly, he echoes María's question, Something wrong. Something wrong, indeed. Nodding, he looks around the kitchen.

Everything, she thinks, everything betrays us. The speed and tone of a voice, the angle of a gaze, the shaking in her leg as she waits for his next words. Can a voice be controlled in every circumstance. Fina should know but Fina is saying nothing. Ernesto's intrusion, the invisible blades he is tossing about the room, prompt her to take her father's arm.

What regiment did you say your husband was with, señora

Vázquez, Ernesto continues, tapping with his knuckles on the wall. I spent a lot of time searching for your husband. Up and down the country. All over the place. You must know. I've been keeping your sister informed of my progress, the time I've been spending on your behalf. He shakes his head in mock sadness. It seems, señora Vázquez, that your husband was never in one of the government's regiments. Isn't that strange, he ponders, moving onto the next wall. Knock knock. How do you explain that.

María looks at her sister but Julita will not return her gaze. What did he whisper to her.

Mamá, Alicia starts to whimper.

Put those things down, Ernesto snaps at his comrades with the mallets. You're frightening the girl. Well... He turns to María. Is there anything you want to tell us. He takes a moment to enjoy her silence before continuing. I have reason to believe there may be something...worthy of investigating in this house. Tapping as he goes.

That's a strange thing to say, she holds her ground. Very strange. You have received our hospitality many times, Ernesto. You know this house well.

Either your husband never joined one of the government's regiments, Ernesto begins answering his own question, in which case he must be somewhere that you know of, or he joined one of the fascist regiments. Which is something you would also know. We will investigate the first of these theories first. It won't take long.

He stops at señora Rojas on her mattress by the stairs. Are you here to fix the windows, the old lady asks from under her blanket.

Move her over there, Ernesto orders his comrades, pointing to where don Millán and Fina are gripping each other by the stove, Fina's free arm around Tomás.

Señora, our apologies, the younger man says, as he and his colleague help the old lady up. The blanket slips. Ay, ay, ay.

You should be ashamed of yourselves, don Millán mutters.

right up to the wall—does he know I'm here or has he come on a hunch

did he guess the secret of this house—or could Julita—no—she'd never

the doctor perhaps—the children—who

knock knock—up—down—as if there was nothing between us—no wall—knock again—louder this time—in my ear knock knock

I'm done for

what's under the stairs he is asking—it sounds hollow

nothing—nothing she repeats—too much anxiety in her voice—I'm a dead man—and my dear María who has risked everything—what will they do to her—to the others

and Julita

I—

I can't—

stop—

shaking—

help me God—the whole house will start vibrating

Nothing. Nothing.

Well, we might as well check it out. Ernesto nods to his comrades. As good a place as any to start, he surmises, now knocking around the entire perimeter of the wall under the stairs.

Strange to close in an empty space, he throws María a questioning look. When was this done.

A long time ag. Her voice clogs in her throat. Ago. Julita stares at her.

Don Millán rouses himself, increasingly outraged. Young man, he raises his voice to the soldier who has taken the first strike at the wall, these are decent people. They have done nothing but protect us since the siege began. We are all Spanish here. You are making a mistake. Whose orders are you acting under.

Sir, you would be well advised to keep your mouth shut, Ernesto interjects. Or are you implicated in this too. Maybe you all are.

Incomprehension. Implicated in what.

Don Millán ignores him. You, sir, have eaten at our table many times. Why are you showing such disrespect to these ladies. They have done nothing but help the Republican govern—

SHUT IT!

Fina squeezes her father's arm, shaking her head in distress.

You too, Ernesto barks at Alicia, who is whimpering louder now.

pounding—against the wall—in my head

how long did I hold my breath back then—the day I escaped—
till my lungs burst

like now

hold my breath—hold—one minute—slow release

and when I could hold no longer they had disappeared—I could
hear the Messerschmitts retreat—and the pounding of shells
grow faint on dry ground—pounding like now

Uribe—you got away lightly—dignified—even with your brains
all over my face

Uribe—help me

Rubble, they have seen. Familiar buildings, friends' houses, Joselito's. But it's different when it's your own home.

Dust, liberated into the air, dances lightly. Oblivious, it floats in rays of light, going nowhere, answerable to no one.

What will happen to him now, María thinks. To all of us. Freedom is such a complicated thing. Maybe under the stairs was freedom. Freer than whatever awaits us. That much is certain now.

A hole in the wall has no colour. Black, perhaps, sucking life from all the colours. Jagged edges, bricks and rubble strewn on the kitchen floor. Plaster flying. The mallet swings with no technique or skill. It swings with brute force.

Some are silent, not knowing what the intruders will find. Some are silent thinking they know what they will find. María is silent because she knows. Did Julita suspect. Did she invite Ernesto to do this in order to save herself once he discovered Ramón was in none of their regiments. She has never understood what goes through her sister's mind. She looks at the children, at Manolo standing with his cousins. It's hard to feel anything now. Not dread. Not despair. Sadness, maybe. Weariness.

Each strike against the wall reverberates around the kitchen. A bigger hole and Ernesto pushes his comrade back, peers in, then stands tall. Well, well, well. What a surprise, he announces. I believe we may have found your husband, señora Vázquez.

Is there someone there, Julita is aghast. Ernesto gives her a contemptuous look. Ernesto, you don't think I expected this… Darling, she gasps. Is it Ramón, she throws a horrified look at her sister.

All eyes on her now. The children, incredulous.

This is your doing, María says quietly to her sister. Whether she told him because she suspected anything or not, she brought Ernesto into the house. She prompted him to search. Almost with pity for Julita, María repeats, Just remember, you brought this on yourself. On all of us.

I haven't done anything, Julita is indignant.

Get him out, Ernesto commands and the pounding resumes.

A part of them wants to rush to the hole to see who is under the stairs. A man, after all. Not the rats señora Rojas was sure she could hear. There was a man under the stairs. Since when.

But no one moves. And no one asks. They are looking at María who with every thwack of the mallet grows weaker. She stumbles to a chair and sits. Alicia clings to her and she wishes she wouldn't, as if she might contaminate the child. If only she could get the children out of the kitchen. Spare them this.

I'm very cold, she tells them. Would you children go upstairs and get my green cardigan. I—

You're going nowhere, Ernesto barks at them. If you open your mouth again, he shouts at María, you'll pay for it. That goes for the rest of you. Yes, you too, he adds for Julita's benefit.

Julita stares at Ernesto. This is not the man she has come to know. He has never shown such contempt for her. Not for anyone. Why is he speaking to her like this.

The hole is big enough for everyone to see a shadow squatting in the corner. Ernesto nods with satisfaction as the men pull him out. Deserter, he accuses calmly as if he expected this all along. Well, fancy that, he mocks María, your beloved husband. What have you to say now.

In response to her silence he scoffs again. Such ingratitude. Typical. But what would you expect of fascists.

Julita looks up. We're not... But her voice trails off because she sees him now.

The children are stunned. What is Papá doing under the stairs. What is uncle doing under the stairs. Was he not... They daren't utter a word.

Julita's blood drains from her face because this is not María's husband even though Ernesto keeps saying it is. This isn't Ramón, she wants to say, but can't.

I can only assume you knew your brother-in-law was hiding here, Ernesto addresses Julita with scorn. Of course you did. How could you not have known. His disdain would cut through her were she not in shock.

Imperceptibly, Julita shakes her head, all energy drained. She tries to say his name but she can't even mouth it. Not even in her mind will it form. An... Anton... Anton...

a river is a living thing—why do I think that now—the river broad and swift muscling through the valley

I would not have thought to lose my footing—not deliberately— life is all you think of—infinite ways of staying alive while you're in hell

so many had fallen—tens of thousands in one day—it is our duty to live

I hear my comrades shouting after me but I flounder—can't breathe—gasp and kick—mud up my nose and in my mouth— splutter—frantic—lose the rifle—lose the pack

barely my hand above the water trying to cling to something— anything

air—I need air

barely my head surfaces and huge I gulp the air and water— cough and choke—feel the water's pull through reeds and slime

sound is muffled but you can tell the difference between the drone of fighter planes and the roar of fast flowing water

just when I thought I would die the river pushed me up and spat me out against a rock

miraculously I clung—saw the branch—pulled myself towards the river bank—enough to wade to the edge

covered in mud I became mud—coughed up mud expecting to

hear artillery—trucks

but the world had gone quiet

in the mud I lay—how long—eternity—spent—until silence became real

ants crawled around me and I knew what I needed to do

crawl—industrious and unobserved—follow the stars Juanjo had so often pointed out

Polaris—like he said—then east

crawl through ditches in the dark—low—worming my way back—low until she found me in the ditch

So many ways it could have turned out, but he never imagined this. He knows what they will do to him. Whether slow or swift it will be nothing compared to the humiliation of this. Paraded in front of them all.

He can't look at Julita. Not at María either. Let the soldiers take him out of here. The quicker the better. He casts a pitiful glance at Manolo as the militiamen drag him out. Son, he wants to say. Forgive me. But nothing comes.

Fear and joy indistinguishable, Manolo attempts to run towards him but Ernesto pushes him back.

No, his father pleads with his eyes.

No one will touch the prisoner. None of you leave the house, Ernesto snaps at the others. A quick hand gesture and one of his men takes up guard over the little group. Outside, he orders the other two, jerking his head towards the door. *Vamos a dar un paseo*, he nods at Antonio. Let's go for a walk.

This skeletal man must be Ramón, don Millán and Fina are shocked. How long was he there. How…

Julita wants to say something, that she knew nothing, that this is not Ramón. But she is numb. Antonio is dead. Was. Drowned. She still has the letter from the Ministry of National Defence. She stares at Ernesto, her gaze following him and the men to the door. Out, they push him. Out, and in the silence she turns to her sister, mouth agape, still speechless. Her sister who is shuddering, tears burning her cheeks.

Through the open door they feel the cold and hear the whirr and blast of distant shells. No one moves or dares to speak except Manolo. Where are they taking him, he asks the man who is guarding them.

It's best if you stay here and don't move, the militiaman advises. Shh..., he adds with a note of consideration in his voice, the same that apologised to señora Rojas.

But the line is blurred between bravery and stupidity, daring and innocence. Manolo, who has never given any thought to these things makes a dash for the door. There are questions he needs answered.

Hey, the man calls, running after him. Come back.

Don't, Manolo, María shouts, but he is already out the door. His mother, mute, as if struck by lightning.

The crack of a gunshot makes them jolt. Hands to ears, they gasp. It can only mean one thing. But who.

Papá, they hear Manolo cry and there is no mistaking, then, what that cry means. He shouts to Ernesto to let him go and in the tumult they hear Ernesto's confusion. Your father, he is asking Manolo, but Manolo isn't interested in Ernesto's questions. Repeatedly he shouts, Papá. In the kitchen they will him to stop shouting, stop struggling. It will only make things worse. But on it goes. Distraught, words they've never heard Manolo use before.

Then whack, a silence, another crack of gunfire. An end to the shouting and now they wish he would shout again to dispel their worst fears. They strain their ears into the silence and all they hear is the crunch of footsteps on snow.

Slowly, dreamily, Julita's body relaxes into stupor, slumps onto the ground. Thud. They stare at her but no one moves.

Señora Rojas looks surprised. Was that thunder, she asks. When no one answers, she smiles. At least the bombs have stopped. Listen, her face brightens. My prayers have been heard.

Seville, 1960

They sit on the terrace in Alicia's house, among orange trees and bougainvillea. Alicia and her family, Tomás and his girls, Grandpa Ramón who always admires the vibrant colours of the south, the miracle of being alive.

Clatter and banter of a usual Sunday lunch and, Finish what's on your plate, Grandpa says to Elena, the little one. You should be grateful for your food. You don't know what it's like to go rummaging in bins for food.

Like when you were in the war, Grandpa, she asks.

That's right. Now finish up.

When Grandma died, her questions continue.

Come on, Tomás urges, cutting the lamb into smaller pieces. Finish up and you can have ice-cream.

Why did Grandma die, Elena asks.

Many people died, her father says. Open wide.

And how did Grandma die.

Tomás repeats the old story. She just walked out of the house one day and never came back. The more he repeats it, the truer it becomes.

Unfathomable, it lingers in her curious mind. Last one, now, Tomás coaxes, open wide.

Just for a moment, it looms. A darkness no one will ever understand.

Alicia thinks of the letters. Vaguely recalls taking them from under the stairs after Ernesto and the militiamen took their mother for a walk with aunty. Then nothing. No recollection of putting them in the box Encarna gave her for the Nativity play. A box intended for myrrh and she smiles because she still has no idea what myrrh looks like.

Once, on holiday home from boarding school, she read some of them, but the words made no sense. Not until she was much older did she understand she should have left them under the stairs. In the dark, with all the other memories and twisted truths.

She looks at her father now. An old man, no longer the man in the letters, his arm around little Manolito, admiring a water pistol with gravitas. He has been a good father. A good grandfather. There's no more to be said.

Acknowledgements

My most heartfelt thanks goes to the members of the Troika writing group (Eamonn Lynskey, Ross Hattaway and Elizabeth McSkeane) for their constant encouragement and invaluable comments.

Elizabeth McSkeane of Turas Press deserves very particular thanks. Her motivation, guidance, patience and professional care have ultimately made this novel possible.

I am grateful to Ross Hattaway for editing and proof-reading. There are not many with his keen editorial eye and his sensitive engagement with the text.

During early research in Spain, I had the good fortune to meet Professor Nigel Townson in Madrid, who was generous in sharing his historical expertise, as well as suggesting much reading material from which many details in the novel are gleaned.

To the Instituto Cervantes in Dublin I owe thanks for their screening of "30 años de oscuridad", an animated film (director, Manuel H. Martín; script, Jorge Laplace; actors, Juan Diego, Luis Fernández de Eribe, Ana Fernández) that narrates the experience of Manuel Cortes, who spent thirty years hidden in his house during and after the war.

My thanks to the librarians and staff at the Military Archives in Avila, and in particular to the staff of the National Historical Archive on the Spanish Civil War in Salamanca for pointing me in the direction of the online newspaper archives.

There are many people who offered me constant support, personal recollections and details of the Spanish Civil War, anecdotes, suggested reading material, the loan of books and of a stethoscope, listening ears, quiet space for writing, and valuable comments on various drafts. They are: Ana and Peter Crowe, Mark Kealy, Rachael Kealy, Bjarke Hellden, Paul Donnelly, Begoña Alvarez, Conor Fennell, Kevin O'Doherty, Geraldine Grimm, Darko Bakić, Annie Crawford, John O'Rourke, Michael Bosonnet, Carmen Sanjulián, Alicia Montañés.

The person to whom I owe my greatest debt of gratitude is my grandfather, José María Serrano Sos. It is because of his involvement in the Spanish Civil War that I have spent much of my life pondering the reasons that might motivate decisions I found hard to accept. I think I understand a little better now, in a Socratic kind of way: the more I know, the more I realise how much I will never really know.

Mark Ulysseas kindly gave excerpts from the novel an airing in his wonderful online journal *Live Encounters*. I am grateful to him, and to Peter O'Neill who curated that April 2020 edition, for their early acknowledgement of my work.

About the Author

Anamaría Crowe Serrano is a poet, translator, and language teacher born in Dublin to an Irish father and a Spanish mother. Her collections of poetry include *Crunch* (2018), *onWords and upWords* (2016), and *Femispheres* (2008). She has translated poetry and fiction from Spanish and Italian. Much of her work to date has been collaborative. *In the Dark* is her first published novel.